AF390820

Farid Mery

The Book of Laila

A Story Starred by Destiny

Saltillo, Coahuila de Zaragoza. Mexico

2024

ISBN-13: 978-2-4987-9249-0

Legal deposit: 1-13816170391

1st edition, septiembre 2024

Print on demand

Printed: On demand

Proofreading by: Farid Mery

Cover design by: Yazmin Mery

Text design and layout by: Rohit Solanki

To Laila. The one from real life.

The one who transcends fiction and geographical, physical and heart barriers.
Thank you for being my muse and for inspiring these chapters.

To all of those who dream of having a love like the ones in books.
Never stop dreaming.

This is not a story about love,

This is a story about fate.

Table Of Contents

FOREWORD
THE RED THREAD

I know that the world keeps turning, that stars die and new suns are born. However, in this cosmic swirl, in this infinite dance of time and space, there exists an invisible thread that keeps us connected. Something that goes beyond the tangible and visible.

We may not be destined to be together in this life, but I know that my love transcends the boundaries of time and space. Though I may not be able to see you physically, you will always be present in my heart and in every corner of my being. And as the world keeps turning, as stars keep dying and new suns are born, our invisible bond will continue to unite our souls, intertwining our destinies in an eternal dance.

There is a thread —imperceptible but powerful— that unites people who are destined to meet, soulmates who search tirelessly for each other in every corner of the world. For some, the thread ceases to be invisible and is dyed in the most powerful red. This is something that only happens to those who pull back the veil from their eyes, to begin to see the signs. Those subtleties that many ignore, but that are everywhere.

Suddenly, you will see the thread wrapping around a memory: a plane ticket you bought, the seat number you got on a flight or train ride, a phone call, a song playing on the radio, a hug, a fleeting encounter, and even the message of a fortune cookie you ignored at the time.

The red thread began to envelop Laila, an enigmatic young woman living in the extravagant city of Dubai. The thread traveled across seas, cultures, landscapes, and languages, and climbed the towering mountains of the Sierra Madre Oriental until it reached Saltillo. Perhaps, in the midst of a colorful "Matlachina" dance held one February, the red thread detached itself from the flowered bandana of a dancer and traveled until it found Elias' home.

The thread, still invisible to him, made him sit down in front of his computer and start organizing a trip that would change his life. They both lived lives separated by vast distances, with cultures and traditions that seemed to separate them even more. But destiny, that great web of coincidences and secrets of the universe, decided to cross their paths in an unexpected way.

It was at an airport where their gazes met for the first time, in the midst of the turmoil and rush of modern life. Their souls vibrated in unison, as if that brief instant in time had submerged them in a sea of unknown emotions. There, in that ephemeral encounter, the red thread of their lives gathered strength and began to become a strong fabric, intertwining their destinies, knotting them together and defying all the conventions of logical and rational love.

Their lives became a delicate dance of coincidences and serendipity. Like pieces of a cosmic puzzle, Laila and Elias found each other without looking for one another, missed each other without having had each other, and loved each other without having touched. The red thread that united them seemed to possess a magnetism of its own, an unstoppable force that guided them toward their inevitable encounter. And love, when true, surpasses the frontiers and difficulties of this earthly world.

Introduction

Two Passengers

يـاما مرتني عيُون وماسهيت إلا بعيونك
"I have passed through many eyes,
but I only got lost in yours."
Mahmoud Darwish

At the Dubai airport, two souls would meet in a magical moment.

Elias had a distinctive hurry in his stride. That specific pace of someone trying to get to his boarding gate at an airport in time. He was juggling to get through the bustling human tide, while dragging his black polycarbonate carry-on with one hand, trying not to spill a drop of the iced espresso coffee he had bought minutes ago. He needed the caffeine to serve as fuel for his body.

Dubai airport is an imposing place that receives millions of passengers and opens the way to contrasts. It is a hive of activity that accommodates people from all over the world on its runways. Almost all passengers are constantly on the move, with conversations intermingling, languages merging, and noises and alarms becoming indistinguishable amidst the bustle. The characteristic sound of luggage wheels against the floor seems to mark a secret rhythm, accompanying those who come to spend a few hours of their day here.

In this place, where personal stories blur among the rushing crowd, two souls would meet in a magical moment. Elias and Laila would seal their destiny when their gazes met in a vast sea of glances, opportunities, stories, and destinies.

Elias found a place to sit and rest while he waited for his flight home, settling into a soft brown leather chair. He took a sip of coffee and pulled his phone out of his pocket.

As he glanced at the screen, he noticed the time and also saw an important notification. The work email he had been waiting for brought back those icy pangs in his stomach, reminiscent of the ones he had felt just minutes ago —when he thought he would be late for his flight—, while rapidly navigating through the modern steel and glass dome that shelters passengers from all over the world.

With his thumb, he touched the screen and opened an email. He hurriedly read through the lines, trying to find the keywords that would give him a general idea of the answer he was waiting for. Bingo! He had found what he was looking for, and in doing so, the pangs left him.

He felt calm and unconsciously celebrated with a sip of iced coffee. He relaxed his body, letting the tension slowly release from his neck, and took a deep breath. Then his thumb went back to fiddling with his cell phone screen. He found Spotify, and among the first options was a song she had recently heard and loved.

He pressed the white circle, and the tune began to play in his wireless headphones, a technological acquisition from his recent time in Turkey. He looked at the clock on the screen. It was 7:10 pm. The masterful beginning of a song called "Júrame," covered by Luis Miguel for his *Romances* album, made him close his eyes for a couple of minutes to concentrate on the moment he was living.

After an unforgettable trip, Elias would return home to Saltillo. Upon his return, he would find himself with a job opportunity that excited him.

Júrame que, aunque pase mucho tiempo

(Swear to me that, even though a lot of time passes)

Nunca olvidaré el momento en que yo te conocí

(I will never forget the moment I met you)

Mírame, pues no hay nada más profundo

(Look at me, because there is nothing deeper)

Ni más grande en este mundo que el cariño que te di.

(Or greater in this world than the love I gave you.)

Elias took his eyes off the cell phone screen and turned his face up. Among the crowd of passengers, he found her. He didn't know her name, what language she spoke, where she was traveling to, or her age. Everything about her was a mystery to him, but something made their eyes meet in a sea of glances. In a place where it was practically impossible to notice the presence of a stranger beyond asking politely (or not) for permission to walk.

He felt something in his stomach again. It wasn't hunger, nor was it caffeine. He found her beautiful, but beyond her obvious beauty, he was struck by the sense of familiarity she aroused in him. "Where do I know her from?" he wondered internally.

The first thing he noticed was that the *hijab* she wore (the veil Muslim women wear to cover their heads) was his favorite color. After locating her, he stopped at her gaze. Her honey-colored eyes, framed by her perfectly outlined eyebrows, served as a window. Without knowing her, he could feel her sweetness and closeness. A face that looked as if painted by some Renaissance artist. He understood that, although he had never seen her face in any other context, she seemed strangely familiar.

She began to walk right up to where he was sitting, and so, as if by those fascinatingly inexplicable quirks of life, the seat next to Elias vacated for her to occupy. He again felt the icy pangs return to his stomach. These last few minutes of his day felt to him to a roller coaster of emotions.

His heart raced and pounded so hard he could hear it thumping inside his temples. His palms became slippery, and his breathing began to feel ragged. Slowly, he took off his headphones and paused the Luis Miguel song that was still playing. He put his cell phone in his pocket and returned the new headphones to one of the compartments of his carry-on luggage.

"It's now or never!" he thought internally. In a drastic impulse, giving no room for rationality to enter the game, he let the words escape from his mouth.

"Nice to meet you."

He could feel his own voice tremble, but she didn't seem to notice. In return for the kind gesture, she responded. They didn't know it at the time, but they both felt as if an electric impulse ran lightly through them from head to toe. As if their souls, after connecting, recognized each other. As if they knew they came from many journeys, from many lives, from many love stories together.

"I'm delighted to meet you too." She replied timidly.

"What's your name?", he asked curiously and thinking up quick, basic questions to keep the conversation from dying.

"My name is Laila."

"Laila," he thought and the name seemed perfect and soothing. Like a delicate and very short melody that now framed that beautiful and mysterious girl in some kind of context. It was the name that would steal his sleep and, later, also his heart.

Then Elias introduced himself, and they both answered the remaining "formal" questions typically exchanged out of courtesy or interest during these encounters. In the next few minutes, Elias learned that she was 28 years old, that she was born in Beirut that she had been residing in Dubai for years, and, fortunately, that she spoke English quite fluently.

He went ahead and also shared some of his personal history. He revealed that he was 32 years old, Mexican, and also came from a Lebanese family. He mentioned recently embarking on an unforgettable trip to Turkey and was now headed back to Saltillo, his hometown in northern Mexico, after receiving a recently confirmed job offer. This position would involve teaching at a prestigious university, a dream Elias had long pursued.

"Turkey?", she asked, impressed. "That's exactly where my family and I are headed next. Then, I plan to return to Beirut to reunite with my grandparents."

Amidst their conversation, Elias and Laila lost track of time. When they finally realized, they almost lost something more: their flights. He was determined not to let her go, even though she would be flying kilometers away from his colorful and warm city.

"Hey," he said uncertainly, "Can I have your phone number?" Laila went blank, unsure of what to do or how to respond. After being paralyzed for seconds, she took Elias's phone from his hands and began to move her thumbs. A smile appeared on her face, captivating her new friend.

Elias took the phone back and saw her contact saved in his address book. With his chest inexplicably feeling heavy, Elias and Laila bid each other farewell. Curiously, they both experienced the same strange, familiar sensation. One that was difficult to describe with words, but now enveloped them. Like rain suddenly appearing to lull the lazy sleep of a Sunday afternoon.

Their gazes met again in one last magical moment before going separate ways. Like two stars in orbit, they embarked on a slow walk towards the boarding gates, submerged in the silent resignation of knowing that each step unstoppably distanced them from one another.

As they progressed, the physical distance widened, but surprisingly, their souls remained intertwined by an imaginary line. It was as if they were connected by an invisible red thread, capable of traversing continents, cultures, time zones, and climates, creating an ethereal bond that defied barriers imposed by tangible reality. The physical separation only intensified the spiritual connection, which, like an intangible bridge, allowed them to feel each other's presence even as they faded from each other's sight.

The kilometers that separated them would cease to matter because now, the bond that began with a random glance and grew with a brief conversation would be stronger than a promise and more ethereal than the most beautiful of dreams. Elias spent the nearly 20-hour flight home thinking about her, looking at the numbers she had written in his phone, as if they were going to tell him personal stories about her.

+961 1 6789364 was the set of digits that, by now, seemed to him like a sort of code to be deciphered in order to connect with this beautiful and mysterious woman. He added a heart (<3) next to her name in the contacts tab of his phone.

Without internet access, he couldn't search for her name in a digital sea of "Lailas" until he stumbled upon her and could see her in a broader context—perhaps at the coffee shop she frequented with her friends, the restaurant she usually visited with her family, or interacting with her pets. He wondered if she would be more of a dog or a cat person, a fan of *tabbouleh* or *fattoush*, or if she might enjoy visiting her grandparents' house to savor the best *Kibbeh Nayeh* ever made.

He closed his eyes and could almost taste the flavor of the perfectly seasoned lamb meat combining with the fragrant smell of the mint leaves that Laila's imaginary grandmother, Jamila, had cut from the home garden.

"Jamila?" he questioned himself. "I'm even making up names for this chick's family now." He couldn't help but chuckle. His mind resembled that of a gifted writer, effortlessly weaving stories with the finesse of an accomplished storyteller. It also resembled the mind of a painter, skillfully mixing colors on his palette to bring his creations to life, or that of an expert sculptor, capable of extracting a unique and sublime piece from a solid block of marble.

In his imagination, he visualized Laila with her honey-colored eyes, gracefully seated on the hood of his truck. She was the central figure in a picturesque scene. They were both immersed in the shared delight of the pink and orange clouds that, with their celestial brushstrokes, painted the Saltillo valley at sunset, creating a scene as idyllic as it was ephemeral.

Captivated by the strength of his own mental creations, Elias closed his eyes and surrendered to the river of stories and fantasies flowing through his mind. In that state of reverie, Laila managed to infiltrate not only his conscious thoughts but also his deepest dreams, weaving a dreamlike realm where their souls danced in harmony. A female voice announcing the plane's arrival in Mexico City snapped him out of his deep dream. He wiped the saliva from his face, organized his belongings, and ran his fingers through his hair. He still had a short journey ahead between the capital and his hometown.

The distance traveled and the passing hours made that encounter with Laila seem like a kind of fantasy. Now Elias' mind abandoned fantasyland and focused, as best he could, on the pending issues he would have to resolve now that he was back home.

Between flights that crossed the skies of different continents, stopovers that marked brief encounters with unknown places, waits that defied patience, and cabs that transported him through the flashing lights of the city, Elias finally arrived at his apartment when the hands of the clock pointed to 5:00 in the afternoon of the following day.

He turned the keys in the lock, and as he opened the door, he was greeted by that unmistakable, comforting smell of "home." This scent, so subjective and personal, has different notes for each individual. For some, home was the cinnamon fragrance that enveloped every corner; for others, it was the smell of food, spices, and garlic that permeated the air. Some identified home with a clean, citrusy scent.

For Elias, however, "home" emanated a unique blend of oak and eucalyptus, an olfactory symphony that instantly transported him to his intimate, personal refuge.

As he stepped through the doorway, he kicked off his boots, letting his bare feet sink into the softness of the foyer carpet. This ritual, so intimate and personal, anchored him back to the everyday, serving as a tangible reminder that, despite the adventures and distances traveled, home was still his safe place within this world.

He set down his luggage with a sigh of relief and poured himself a glass of water. Each sip had the unique taste of the familiar, as if the water itself was telling him stories of his own home, these few square meters in which he felt confident, powerful, and secure.

He plopped down on the black leather sofa, immersing himself in the comfort that only one's own living space can offer. Almost by inertia, he moved his arm to the right, picked up the remote control, and turned on the huge television.

The sound of a Netflix series became the perfect complement, filling the room with electronic whispers that competed with the soft hum of the city filtering through the window. He closed his eyes, feeling his body tired but comforted by the familiarity that surrounded him. However, in the serenity, a sudden "ping" coming from his cell phone broke the stillness, bringing him back to the immediate reality of his living room.

Laila <3_ 5:13 pm

Hello Elias. It's Laila.

How was your trip back home?

Elias experienced how emotion gripped his chest, triggering a cascade of internal questions. How was this possible? He paused for a moment to reflect, surprised by the fact that he didn't remember giving her his phone number.

Uncertainty hung in the air, weaving a mystery that added an additional layer of intrigue to this chance encounter. Were there invisible connections that transcended conventional exchanges of information? These questions mingled with the excitement that throbbed in his chest, creating a cocktail of wonder and curiosity that only intensified the mystery of this fleeting connection.

Chapter one

The Past

أنتِ القصة اللي ما بدياها تخلص

"You are the story I don't want to see end."

Laila's journey

Laila was born in Lebanon, in Beirut, specifically in an area near the sea called Raouche. The mention of this geographical detail made Elias dive even deeper into Laila's mental narrative. He visualized her early years in more detail, imagining her pedaling her bicycle along the famous boardwalk, surrounded by palm trees, salt, and sunsets that tinged the sky with pastel hues. Elias' fanciful thoughts became a kind of movie, where the concrete sidewalks of Raouche became silent witnesses to the childhood of the girl with a Lebanese heart.

The characteristic scent of the sea—iodine, seaweed, brine, and seafood—combined with the warm summer sun, became the essence that made Laila feel at home. This was the smell of "home" to her. This connection with her homeland, though now distant, kept the flame of her identity alive and the roots of her Lebanese heart firmly planted.

However, life had its own plans, and Laila's family found themselves compelled to change course. Her father, Hassan, an architect with remarkable works that captured investors' attention, saw opportunities in Dubai's economic and social growth in the 1990s. This drastic change led the family to pack their bags, leaving behind their home in Beirut and carrying with them a kaleidoscope of memories that would forever linger within those walls upon turning the lock.

Jamila, Laila's maternal grandmother, along with her husband Omar, chose to stay in the now-empty family home, demonstrating their stubbornness and deep attachment to the land. This decision highlighted the contrast between resistance to change and the willingness to venture into the unknown. Although the house stood empty, their hearts remained open to welcome their family whenever they came to visit

The passage of time became more noticeable from a distance. Jamila bid farewell to Laila as a child and witnessed her return the following summer as a young woman.

Laila's childhood and adolescence were forged in this new and promising place, Dubai, which, though eccentric and novel, became her home. The city, with its vibrant colors, imposing sites, and diverse customs, left an indelible mark on her being.

It didn't take long before she and her family fell in love with Dubai, and enveloped by this new atmosphere that soon felt like their own, years passed, and Laila transformed into a beautiful woman, in the eyes of the place that welcomed her.

Laila stood in front of the long mirror in her room. She looked at herself, as if ensuring everything was in place before leaving. She was about to embark on a family trip that excited her. The first destination: Turkey. She was not only excited about visiting a country where the ancient Greek, Persian, Roman, Byzantine, and Ottoman empires converged, but also about the return journey. They would spend a few days in her native Beirut. A visit to her maternal grandmother Jamila was all she needed to make her heart feel full after a trip promising adventures.

A notification from her cell phone informed her that the driver she had hired through a mobile app would arrive shortly. Her family usually assigned her these tasks as her parents were not technologically savvy.

A sensation of slight nervousness ran through her body. Excitement had prevented her from sleeping well the night before. Her honey-colored eyes looked somewhat tired. Laila touched the dark circles under her eyes, trying to disguise them with concealer. Unlike most times when she was at home, her hair was loose. She played with it, running her fingers through the lush dark brown locks. She tied it up as usual and took her *hijab* to cover her head and neck. Looking at herself one last time in the mirror, she felt ready. Prepared for the adventure.

Once again, the sound of her cell phone interrupted her brief encounter with her reflection. The driver announced his arrival. Laila yelled, signaling everyone to leave the house.

"Sabḥ al-Khair! (Good morning!)" she greeted with a warm smile as she settled into the back seat of the car. Laila didn't know it, but with a smile, she could achieve whatever she set her mind to. Her face was generous, and her kind gestures told a story beyond her obvious beauty. Her eyes were a window to her noble heart. She was a sensitive girl, so turning them into a sea was not very complicated.

She was not afraid to cry or express her emotions, whether good or "bad." Because if there was one thing she had learned in years of reading and searching for personal, emotional, and spiritual growth, it was that there was no such thing as a negative emotion. Even anger must be experienced to the fullest. That's why that very famous Pixar movie about emotions was among her favorites.

As the driver took them to the airport, Laila took advantage of the car ride to review her travel itinerary.

She had researched a lot about Turkey, especially Istanbul, the city she would visit. She was excited to get lost in the narrow streets of the Grand Bazaar, explore the majesty of the Blue Mosque, Hagia Sophia, and cross the Bosphorus Bridge. She had also scheduled one of those famous hot air balloon rides, though the idea of waking up early on vacation didn't excite her much.

Laila's visual mind immersed itself in a photo of her grandmother Jamila, found in her cell phone gallery. This small act connected her with the nostalgia and anticipation of the reunion. Just like Elias, who, months later, would discover that he shared with Laila this ability to create mental images, anticipating memories not yet experienced in real life.

He had done the same, searching the internet for images that spoke of Raouche, the land of this girl who unexpectedly shook him up, to help his brain compose memories he had not yet experienced.

A few months later, after the encounter at the airport, they would understand they had this in common. This, and a long list of things that made them seem like "soulmates."

In that exciting conversation where they would discover so many things that made them alike, Elias would interrupt to explain that he had once read that the myth of "soulmates" was not as romantic as people often imagined it.

"So, Elias, how does the topic of soulmates work?" she said with a hint of laughter in her voice.

"Well, you see…" He continued, explaining in his characteristic way of speaking that it was all Aristophanes' fault.

And it was because this ancient Greek playwright was to blame for us spending life waiting to find the other half of our hearts.

The story wasn't a funny invention of Elias, although it seemed so; this was a fact he had recorded in the dialogue called *The Symposium*. Several thinkers and scholars were having dinner. So, to give an intellectual theme to that meal, each one had to offer a speech about love.

The moment for Aristophanes arrived. But there was a problem. The numerous jugs of wine he had drunk that night caused his diaphragm to begin involuntarily contracting. A bout of hiccups crashed the dinner.

"What do I do now?" the thinker asked himself inwardly, and as happens to these men illuminated by wisdom; an answer came to his mind. The muse had once again enlightened him to save him from such humiliation. His story would have to be so compelling that the diners would be absorbed by the narration, forgetting the hiccup accompanying the storyteller.

He began to speak and invent a myth that sought to explain the feeling of loneliness that leads us to cling to the idea that somewhere in the world and at some specific moment, a perfect protagonist, made to our measure, will appear in the pages that narrate the novel of our life, who will accompany us for the rest of the plot.

So, Aristophanes wanted more attention and began to explain how primitive man had a different physiognomy: androgynous creatures, round, with two faces, four arms, and four legs. But despite seeming like characters from a Captain Nemo adventure, created by Jules Verne, these were powerful and fast beings, so much so that the gods began to fear they could be overthrown.

Thus Zeus, who was not foolish, began to notice a plot being woven against Olympus and ordered Apollo to "cut them in half." Then each human being was left as an incomplete entity with two hands, two legs, and one head. Not only had this primitive man been reduced in the number of limbs, but he would be marked (forever) with the need to find his other half. An action in which he would spend his entire life.

Laila would add with her marked Middle Eastern accent when speaking English: —I believe Aristophanes was wrong and that the first man had many heads and many pairs of hands and feet.

"How?" Elias asked. She explained that by cutting them, many humans would seek a way to be together again.

"Not only does the concept of soulmates exist as romantic love. I feel that your entire environment, that network of people you love and who love you back, in a way are also your other halves."

Laila's explanation enchanted Elias, who went from being an active speaker to an attentive listener. She spoke to him about romantic love and the interpretation given to it in Islam. Although Elias's father was of Arab descent, he lived too far from the Middle East to be too religious or practicing. He preferred the "Latinized" and Westernized version that reinterprets the religion of his lineage and adapts it to something more local.

Laila got distracted. She noticed that in person, she could detail Elias much better. He had thick eyebrows, a slanted gaze, almond-toned skin, and a thick, long beard, which was the envy of many of his friends who couldn't even grow a respectable mustache on their faces.

In that conversation that had not yet happened, Laila would tell him how she interpreted love as a divine gift, as God had created men and women to love and care for each other. Which, logically, guarantees the happiness of the couple.

"If you take care of me and dedicate yourself to making me happy, and I do the same for you, love becomes a less selfish act and, as a result, we both end up favored and happy," Laila explained. "Loving is a responsibility. In my eyes, it looks like a long-term commitment. I believe that lovers must be committed to building a strong and lasting relationship."

But enough of jumping ahead to the future. Better to return to the past, to the taxi, to the road to the airport in Dubai, to the photo of Grandma Jamila, and that reunion that would fill Laila's heart. Because for her, her maternal grandmother was also part of that primitive man with multiple heads that Apollo separated, and that's why, despite the distance, she felt powerfully connected to her.

She remembered her when she smelled freshly ground cardamom, mixed with vanilla essence, and if she closed her eyes, she could almost feel the slightly sweet perfume of the spray she used to tame her long mane. The same one that time had tinged with gray and that her granddaughter was capable of sniffing when she hugged her tightly because Jamila was a few centimeters shorter in height than Laila. And it seemed that, over the years, she was shrinking.

Laila found the photo in her gallery from the last time they had seen each other. She checked the date: August 2018. Exactly four long years had passed, a pandemic, and many stories that were owed and would surely be told over coffee served in those porcelain bowls, so characteristic of her grandparents' house and with that particular flavor that the copper gave to the hot drink. Afternoons at her grandparents' house tasted like coffee, cold water, and dates.

The memory of her homeland awakened mixed feelings in Laila. Although she had grown accustomed to life in Dubai and felt at home there, there was always a part of her that longed for the beaches of Lebanon, the warmth of the people, that boardwalk, and the aroma of the markets. The smell of "home," but above all, the scent that reminded her of a happy childhood.

The journey to the airport passed quickly, and before she knew it, Laila was on the plane to Istanbul. During the flight, as she gazed at the clouds from the window, her mind wandered between memories of her childhood in Beirut and the exciting adventure awaiting her in Turkey.

A few hours later, the plane landed smoothly at the Istanbul airport.

Elias's journey

Elias was born in Saltillo and there, sheltered by the mountains that guard the valley, he was raised and grew up. His father passed down to him his sparse Arab customs, his thick beard, and his palate almost shielded against the strong flavors of spices. His mother was Mexican, so Elias was also protected from the effects of the most potent spicy foods. He could eat anything, and for this reason, there was no better plan for him than to gather with his friends and grill some meat over the fiery coals.

The color of burning charcoal, the sound of someone opening a cooler and reaching into a tower of ice to find the cold metal of a canned soda, the smell of roasting meat, and the aromatic puffs of a hookah were the best way to describe his weekends.

Elias felt a great fascination for cooking. What captivated him about this hobby was the ability to show affection through what his hands prepared. To please tastes and cravings, and then to rejoice in hearing from his diners how delicious his dishes were.

He took it seriously. He had a collection of aprons that had grown with his travels, as at each stop, he would buy one with details alluding to the destination he visited. He had invested in professional knives, sharpening steels to keep them sharp, cutting boards, pots, pans, and every utensil he could find. It was logical that he would go crazy, like a child in an amusement park, when he arrived at the kitchen department of a store.

From Monday to Friday, his routine was woven with the rhythm of the pages of books that, strategically chosen, kept him abreast of global events, thus nourishing his tireless quest for knowledge in the field of international relations. Those volumes became his faithful companions, unfolding before him the intricate workings of international dynamics and the complexities of global politics.

His aspirations, focused with determination on a dream that shone like a beacon on his horizon, were to become a university professor. To achieve this, he had meticulously completed all the paperwork and procedures necessary to apply for a coveted position at the Saltillo campus, belonging to the renowned Universidad of Valle de Mexico. This prestigious academic center represented not only a place to transmit knowledge but also the stage where he hoped to sow the seed of understanding and passion for international relations in the youngest and most fertile minds, which were eager for learning.

His purpose went beyond a simple career; he longed to impart knowledge specifically to students of the bachelor's degree in international commerce and business. This choice not only reflected his deep commitment to the discipline but also his desire to contribute to the development of trained professionals aware of the complexity of the global commercial environment. Every day, as he immersed himself in his work, he prepared not only to teach but also to inspire future generations to understand, question, and actively participate in the international stage.

But while eagerly awaiting the realization of that dream, Elias found an unexpected but enriching source of satisfaction leading the association of vendors at a well-known flea market. This role not only provided him with a great deal of fun but also immersed him in a vibrant and diverse world, strengthening his ties with his community.

Heading the dynamic network of vendors at La Guayulera Market, Elias not only became a skilled negotiator and connoisseur of collectible toys, furniture, second-hand clothing, and culinary delights but also became a privileged witness to the stories and solidarity rooted in the people of "his town."

Daily interaction with these traders gave him a practical education about the cultural richness hidden behind each object and in the shared experiences among those lively streets. He understood from experience that what is trash to some can be a precious treasure to others. And this idea about perceptions seemed divinely fascinating to him.

Each day at the market offered him a new lesson in empathy and appreciation for diversity. He found himself not only as a leader of the association but also as a human bridge between the diverse worlds converging in La Guayulera, blending a passion for business with a genuine interest in people and their stories.

This chapter in his life not only taught him about the intrinsic value of objects but also about the richness of the human connections formed around them.

Elias cherished on a shelf in his room several toy dinosaurs, just a few centimeters tall, which he bought on one of his many visits to the market. The brontosaurus on the shelf, sometimes covered in dust, did not know that in a few months it would leave its usual place to travel kilometers to Dubai.

Elias knew them all, from Don Fermin, "the homemade shaved ice guy," with his cowboy hat, to the gamer who had a stand where Elias always left a good portion of his earnings.

One Sunday afternoon at the market, under the warm sun at five in the afternoon, Elias had an idea. Like a kind of epiphany or, probably, a glitch in the connections of his brain after enduring that heat. In the distance, at one of the itinerant stalls of those vendors, he saw a vintage tourism poster.

A sunset bathed in an imperial golden hue the dome of the great Hagia Sophia Mosque and its neighbor, the Blue Mosque. At their feet, colorful buildings merged in perfect symbiosis. It was not clear where one began and the other ended. And to top it off, a dreamlike landscape: the serene waters of the Bosphorus, with blue that flirted with anyone.

On that dream landscape, a Helvetica typeface (used to exhaustion in the sixties) exposed: "Istanbul." Enchanted by that photo, Elias spoke to himself silently. "This is the destination of my next trip." Like pieces of a gear that fit together, this moment of epiphany would lead him to Turkey and also end up guiding him to Laila. She, who shone with a light even brighter than the captivating sunset of the sixty's tourism ad.

Upon arriving home, he sat in front of his computer and bought the tickets. That's how he was, determined when an idea got into his head... No matter how absurd it seemed. He noted in his agenda that he would spend the first days of August in those lands that stretched across Eastern Europe and Western Asia.

Time flew by, and before he knew it, he was having breakfast on the terrace of his hotel in Istanbul. In the background, he had the impressive and imposing domes of the Hagia Sophia and the Blue Mosque. The sky was clear blue, and he could see white seagulls flying high. The pine trees were lush. Green. Fresh.

He looked down, and on his plate, he found dates, classic dried apricots, olives of all colors, sizes, and flavors, pickles, walnuts, pita bread, and cheeses and sausages. It was certainly different from what he ate at home, but it smelled delicious, and he was already accustomed to these strong but captivating flavors.

The hotel he had chosen was not extravagant, but it was comfortable and had a privileged location. It had its charm, so the photos he found on a popular lodging website captivated him. It was nice to find that the place looked just like those photographs promised. One of the many prayers a traveler makes.

He spent those August days tasting new flavors that delighted his palate, discovering places that amazed him, listening to stories, admiring architecture and monuments that took his breath away, learning, absorbing, and letting some of this culture permeate him to make him a much more complete version of himself.

He wanted to blend in with every trip; he wanted to learn, understand, and take from each place what would favor his personal growth, his spirituality, and his way of seeing the world.

He didn't want to collect stamps in his passport or take photos that would be stored in some forgotten digital album. Elias wanted to transform himself, as much as possible, through these places he visited, the people he met, and the new flavors he tasted.

Traveling was for him a poem in motion, a symphony of discoveries that caress the soul. Beyond the boundaries of the familiar horizon, travel spreads its wings and invites to dance with the wonders of the world. With each step, the pages of history unfold before the eyes of the curious traveler. Every corner of the planet whispers lessons that classrooms could never match.

In the journey, the senses awaken to the richness of diversity: the intense colors of bustling markets, the intoxicating aroma of unknown spices, the melodious sound of languages that get lost in the air. Each encounter, whether with history carved in stone or with hearts beating in a local market, enriches the fabric of understanding. Geography becomes a teacher, and maps become canvases on which new stories are drawn.

The importance of traveling lies in the openness of the mind, in the ability to unlearn in order to relearn. In each journey, the traveler becomes a student of the world, a seeker of that truth hidden in the vastness of human experience. Travel is the classroom where empathy flourishes, where differences become bridges, and similarities become embraces.

Thus, each kilometer traveled is a page written in the book of authenticity, a lesson that goes beyond the confines of textbooks.

For this reason, Elias's adventures ended up being lessons, and when he was reflective and immersed in his own inner self on some afternoon at the gym or while driving through the streets of Saltillo, he realized what had happened, and that train he had missed and that had made him angry, turned into a divine gift.

And it was because in his adulthood, he had become a person capable of truly understanding that "everything happens for a reason" and that misfortunes can also be blessings in disguise.

Perhaps this explained that effervescent spontaneity with which he lived. Because, possibly, he let himself be carried away understanding that, at the end of the day, everything would have a reason for being, and he would always be in the right place at the right time.

It had been like this philosophy of life, destiny, chance, impulsiveness, or the red thread, put him at the airport in Dubai at the right moment. The adventure through Turkey had come to an end, and this strategic stopover at the emirate's airport would give him an adventure more exciting than any he had lived before.

Chapter Two

The Distance

"To be or not to be with you is the measure of my time."

Jorge Luis Borges

Elias couldn't believe his eyes. Faced with the mystery, he decided to cut to the chase:

Elias _ 02:17 am

Hi Laila, how are you? It must be early in the morning there. I have two questions for you: What are you doing awake? And how do you have my number? 😂

Laila <3_ 05:23 pm

Hahaha...

I'm awake because I slept
for almost the entire five-
hour flight. I have the
superpower of sleeping on
planes.
The second question will
remain a mystery that I may
tell you about one day.

Even though he hated not being able to solve the enigma of the phone number and knew that the thought would torment him for days, Elias couldn't help but smile just imagining future conversations.

Days turned into weeks and weeks into months. Elias and Laila didn't let 24 hours go by without talking to each other. They were each other's virtual companions. Even though the clock ticked relentlessly, not even the ten hours that separated their time zones could distance them.

As she drifted off to sleep, he stayed awake, longing for the dawn that would bring his virtual friend back to him. A new day, not yet marked on the calendar, awaited them both.

Over the course of that month, their WhatsApp exchanges increased dramatically, weaving a digital connection that defied space and time. Across their screens, more than a thousand files traveled back and forth: photos capturing fleeting moments, videos filled with laughter and emotions, movies suggesting alternate worlds, quotes that stayed with them, and even Instagram and TikTok posts that somehow made them feel closer.

Aware of the importance of their connection, Elias pinned the conversation to the top of his chat list —a symbolic gesture reflecting her priority in his digital life. In a spontaneous act of reciprocation, she did the same, sealing a silent promise to always be present on each other's screens, even when words weren't needed.

Elias _

I was invited to a friend's wedding on Saturday. I couldn't help but fantasize about you going with me. I can picture us arriving, looking our best.

Laila <3_ 05:23 pm

That's funny. I was also invited to a wedding this weekend.

Saturday slipped into the afternoon hours, and as Elias perfected the details of his beard and immersed himself in a YouTube tutorial to master the art of tying a perfect knot in his emerald green tie, his phone interrupted the ritual with a familiar notification. Although he didn't need to look at the screen to confirm the identity of the sender, he opened the conversation and was greeted by the radiant sight of Laila absorbed in the midnight celebration. It was a photo she had shared with him.

Her *hijab* and dress, magnificent and delicate, shared the same shade that he had carefully selected for his tie. The harmony of the colors wove a symbolic bond, an echo of connection that went beyond written words.

Elias _

Look at this! We're even matching.

Elias fiddled with his phone's camera, deleting several photos before finally sending a selfie to Dubai. The picture captured his emerald green tie against the crisp white of his formal shirt.

He entered the hall and scanned the faces of the guests until he spotted his best friend Roberto. Elias weaved through tables, decorations, waiters, and the occasional guest to reach him. This tall man, with thick black hair and glasses, received him with open arms. Elias could't hold back and felt confident enough to share his news.

"Beto, I think I'm in love."

"Whoa there, slow down. This calls for a toast first". Roberto said, signaling to a waiter.

As Elias watched the bartender fill a small glass cup with tequila for his friend, whom he loved like a brother, tension coiled in his stomach. Beads of sweat began to break out on his forehead, and the emerald green tie suddenly felt like a rope constricting his breathing.

"Cheers!" Roberto said to Elias, who instead of wine preferred to toast with a glass filled with ice, sparkling water, and a lemon peel. Not drinking alcohol always made him uncomfortable at these events, especially with the need to explain his choice. But he knew his good friend wouldn't question it. So, he toasted confidently, the urgency to confess building in his chest. The absurdity of the situation struck him, and a smile played on his lips.

"*Cabrón* What? Are you already laughing all by yourself?" Roberto asked, confused.

"More or less." Elias replied, letting out a liberating laugh.

He did his best to shout keywords over the loud music, managing to tell Roberto about his adventure at the Dubai airport and the mysterious girl with bright eyes who traveled more than thirteen thousand kilometers every night to visit him in his dreams.

Perhaps, in some alternate universe, the ever-practical Roberto would have advised Elias to abandon this wild goose chase and focus on courting "the blonde girl from the corner and her friend, the one in the pink dress." They probably wouldn't have even had this conversation. Perhaps they might have ended the night with the blonde and her friend.

Maybe the music, the excitement of the event, and the late hour would have made Roberto forget Elias's story altogether, only to ask him to repeat it the next morning. Perhaps. Probably. Maybe. This time, however, everything seemed to align, making even the slightest possibility feel like a certainty.

So, Roberto, who was as good a party buddy as he was an advisor, unleashed his eloquence and empowered Elias to pursue love. No matter the cost, Elias would have to pack his heart in a metaphorical suitcase and travel to bridge the ten-hour difference that separated him from her.

That day was different. Elias spent the wedding chatting with his friend, sharing moments with acquaintances, and imagining a future with Laila while enjoying the bride and groom's first dance from the front row.

The first chords of Unchained Melody filled the air, sung by the powerful voices of Il Divo. This Italian cover of the song made famous by the Righteous Brothers in 1965 drew all the guests towards the dance floor.

Both Elias and Laila knew and remembered the song from the movie Ghost. For Laila, it was a chick-flick she watched as an adult, part of her personal mission to see most of the 90s movie classics. For Elias, it was a movie he snuck in to watch as a child, hidden from his parents because it was deemed "a movie for adults."

The bride and groom danced with the sunset as their backdrop, bathed in a golden light that ignited Elias's imagination. He wasn't alone. Many other single guests used this moment to yearn for the future day when they would dance "their song."

Elias felt his phone vibrate inside his jacket pocket. Checking it, he saw a WhatsApp notification. Laila let him know she had arrived home. He replied wishing her good night and sweet dreams, a strange feeling washing over him as he realized her night was ending just as his was truly beginning.

Laila and Samia reached the mountain peak together, sharing not only the physical challenge but also the deep connection unique to sisters. The seven-year gap between them had fostered in Laila an admiration that, since childhood, was woven with threads of respect for her older sister, who represented a kind of maternal figure. Samia, at 35, was a married woman and mother of three. The family she had built with Karim became a beacon of inspiration for the young protagonist of this story.

The getaway to Chabrouh Dam, located about 40 kilometers northeast of Beirut, became a special chapter in the last days of the family trip. The sisters ventured out together, exploring the captivating landscapes that surrounded the dam. The vastness of the reservoir seemed to reflect the breadth of Samia's dreams and aspirations, who shared stories of how beautiful and peaceful this place was, a place she'd always wanted to visit.

Every corner of Chabrouh Dam became a meeting point between tradition and modernity, a tangible testimony to the cultural and natural wealth that embraced the region. At that moment, the mountain not only supported their steps but also the indelible connection between two souls united by blood and a sisterly love that was capable of overcoming anything.

The walk was livened by numerous jokes and memories. The goal was to climb a famous rock at the top of the dam to be able to take a picture together for the memory, which would frame an incomparable background. Before achieving the ascent, Samia could see herself printing the photograph with Laila and looking for a nice frame to place it in the living room of her house. A space that in decorative terms was one of her greatest prides.

She also thought about giving a copy to her sister and surprising her with a gift that had sentimental value.

The calm blue color of the water was impressive and contrasted with the rocks, which seemed to be made of clay among which some plants had crept in to give a touch of green to the already celestial scenery. The rock formations seemed to be cut with millimeter precision, but the truth is that, of this visual spectacle, nature had all the credit.

"I missed this. Being able to be together." Samia said, as she placed her hand on her younger sister's shoulder.

"Me too." Laila replied, controlling her emotions so that nostalgia would not escape and take full control of the situation, making her cry.

After reaching the summit, the girls waited patiently for a few tourists to finish taking photos on the famous rock. Finally, with the area clear, they seized their moment to capture a picture and preserve the memory of their adventure.

Laila walked on the rock, a kind of natural diving board, and sat on the cold and humid surface to wait for Samia, who was in charge of the technical and photographic work. She took her cell phone and with the camera, captured her sister. She was captivated by Laila's pose, her thoughtful face, her deep gaze and that incomparable natural background.

That day, Laila had dressed in black: sports shoes and cotton Lycra for comfort, matching hijab and cap to protect her face from the sun. Since she had learned about the daily use of sunscreen and skin care routines through the internet, her face looked like porcelain. Taking care of it, seeing the results, was now a priority every time she was exposed to the sun.

For a moment she looked to the side, enjoying the view offered by the cozy town of Faraya. During the ascent, she had heard a guide explaining to his group of tourists that the name that baptized the place came from the Phoenician and meant "the land of fruits and vegetables."

It made sense to her, since the greenness that welcomed hundreds of crops was captivating. In seconds she thought she would have loved to see this place, from this rock on which she sat, when it is covered with snow in winter.

She made a promise to herself: "One day I will come to sit here with the love of my life, to see the snowy village." Suddenly her sister's voice pulled her out of her internal dialogue and her fantasies. With a gesture and a smile, she invited her to step aside so that she could also sit on the rock. Minutes before, Samia had improvised a tripod between some stones and programmed the timer on her phone's camera so that they could appear together in the picture.

Samia's phone camera took over 20 automatic photos. When she got up to review them, she found several snapshots that captivated her. —Laila, you're going to love this photo I took of you! I'm pretty sure you'll love it so much that it will become your next profile picture."

She turned back to where her sister was standing and smiled at her. She got up, shook the dirt off her body and hands, and walked over to confirm if that photo was worth posting.

Samia showed her masterpieces to her little sister and in the midst of silence and surrounded by wonderful nature, she blurted out a question that had been stuck between her lips since the family vacation began.

"Sister! Who's this person you are talking to so much on the phone?"

The question made Laila go from feeling quite hot to almost shivering with cold. She didn't know what to answer, so she improvised a little lie.

"Who? You are just being paranoid. I'm chatting with my friends. We have a very fun WhatsApp group and they are enjoying my trip adventures."

After the walk, the sisters returned to their grandparents' house to rest, get ready and go out again, now with the whole family, to the Al Falamanki restaurant, in its Raouche branch. They chose it because it had beautiful sea views, a good family atmosphere, backgammon boards and, according to Samia, they prepared the best *shanklish* served with quinoa and kale.

Hassan and Dalida, Laila's parents, accepted the proposal and invited Omar and Jamila to complete the group.

Later that night, Samia couldn't stop thinking about her sister's sudden relationship with the phone screen. She had her sitting next to her and very close, but she didn't dare question her again. She didn't expect that, when she turned her gaze, she would notice that Laila was sending the photograph to a certain guy named "Elias". So, she didn't hesitate to start her attack, loaded with questions.

"So... Are you going to be real now and confess to me who this mysterious Elias is that has you with your head in your cell phone?" She said discreetly so as not to attract the attention of the other family members. There were ten people sitting at that table.

Laila looked at Samia with anguish, but her older sister's gaze greeted her with such warmth that, without saying a single word, they knew that between them there was a safe space to speak the truth. Laila went into the photo gallery, searched quickly with her fingers and found her favorite photo of him. She zoomed in and shared it with Samia. The image showed Elias, a young man with kind eyes and a warm smile, standing in front of a breathtaking mountain landscape. The background looked vaguely familiar.

While Laila's sister peppered her with questions, trying to get every single detail squeezed out of her, she noticed a message from him pop up on her screen.

Elias _

Your photo is almost
perfect. You are very lucky
to have a country with such
beautiful places.

Laila was thrilled. She loved receiving compliments about Lebanon, because she loved her country. She read the message about seven times and while she kept the conversation with Elias open, in front of her eyes, she received a photo. The photo showed Elias rappelling down a mountain, his helmet, gloves, and harness sparkling in the golden sunlight. The lush vegetation around him was so green that it matched his camouflage jacket. He had also started his day climbing mountains and hiking.

He wasn't alone. He had joined Roberto and a group of adventurous friends to explore the natural beauty of El Chiflón, a canyon with a waterfall on the border between Saltillo and General Cepeda. Without a doubt, this was an oasis in the middle of the desert.

They agreed on something, besides the activity, and that is that they both promised to take each other to these charming places someday.

Laila <3_
Well, I would love to visit
Mexico. Especially that
mountainous place that
Looks so beautiful.

                Elías_
                Even though we are very,
                very, very far away… I feel
                As if you were close. As if,
                if it were possible, we
                were together today. First
                in Lebanon and then here
                in el Chiflón

Chapter Three

We'll Always Have... Dubai?

"I have late night conversations with the moon; he tells me about the sun, and I tell him about you."

S. L. Gray

When Ilsa Lund asks Rick Blaine what will happen to them when she boards that plane, he answers with one of the most memorable lines in cinema: "We'll always have Paris."

Thus, the film *Casablanca* (1942) concludes. In black and white, with glassy eyes and dressed in the memorable trench coats and those hats made in the Piedmont region of Italy, the characters convey a deep sense of loss.

Rick explains to her that the moments they shared can never be erased, no matter the miles of distance that separate them.

And so, like the unforgettable characters of *Casablanca*, who in the midst of the uncertainty and turbulence of World War II uttered the emblematic phrase "we'll always have Paris," the love story of this book is also woven with those timeless moments that resist the passage of time. It is as if each shared moment were a jewel in the necklace of memory, shining with the light of nostalgia.

Although in this case there were no kisses shared, no intertwined hugs or words spoken aloud, the essence of what could have been —their unfulfilled dreams— remains alive in the secret corners of their hearts.

The nights that were lengthened by the absence of the other, the destinations they never explored together, the projects that were left unfinished, all of this becomes a testament to what could have been, but which, despite their physical absence, remains present in the plot of this story. Paris, in this context, stands as a symbol of those intangible moments that endure in the heart, a city that encapsulates the magic of "that" which was and will not be repeated.

In this journey through the labyrinth of memories, each Parisian Street becomes a corridor of memory, each corner is an echo of laughter not shared, and each monument stands as a silent witness to the promises that were never spoken. It is as if, in some corner of eternity, the spirit of Paris acts as a beacon that illuminates the paths of what could have been.

Although fate has dictated that Elias and Laila would not share the same physical spaces, the reality is that they would always have their own Paris, a metaphor for the dreams not fulfilled and the horizons they have not explored together.

In each melancholy sunset, in each song that reminds them of what was not, the promise resounds that, despite all the losses and goodbyes, the memories will persist as an immortal treasure. Because in the vast canvas of their lives, Paris is not just a city, it is a state of mind, a constant presence that beautifies the landscape of what could have been.

"There's something you never told me." Elias said to Laila as they walked along the streets over the canals of the Dubai Marina. The faint sounds of splashing water and children's laughter carried away by the breeze that filled the air.

"What haven't I told you?"

"How did you get my phone number?"

"It's amazing that you never forgot it," she said with timid laughter, as if now that she was in front of him, shyness dominated her a little more than usual. "It's very easy," she continued to explain "when I took your cell phone to write down my contact information, I dialed my own number. As soon as the call came in, I hung up from your phone, and then when I checked my missed call history... There you were, Elias Mansour Ramos.”

“And...”

“Before you interrupt me to ask how I know your full name. It’s because I have internet skills. So yes, I admit that I investigated you. There is a CIA side of me you will get to know.”

Elias and Laila walked bathed in the warm glow of the sunset, with Samia following a few centimeters behind. The designated chaperone decided to give her little sister some space (just a little) to have a private conversation with this boy who had made a very good first impression on her and with whom, in a way, she had also already established a kind of virtual relationship.

He couldn’t stop looking around and contemplating that landscape that seemed as colossal as it was surreal. He was in Dubai, thousands of miles from his very own little desert, the place where he felt at home. Everything was huge, wide, magnificent; everything smelled different and looked illuminated by another light. But besides all that, he had Laila by his side. He could smell her perfume, he could get a sense of her, he had front-row tickets to her reactions, he could listen to her and look at her.

A good friend had already warned him about some “protocols” he should follow to make a good impression and not to overstep the boundaries. Knowing this information, for which he was grateful, may have made him act more stiff than usual. If the situation was already edgy, adding the factor of the required distances made the atmosphere more tense. So much so that Elias could swear that that day he could feel and measure the atmospheric pressure.

However, the conversation began to flow, and with each dialogue that received an answer, the tension began to dissipate, and the bodies of both began to shed their stiffness and feel in a pleasant and natural state of relaxation.

"I can't believe I can look him in the eye", Laila thought as she smiled and abstracted herself from Elias' dialogue, to feel infinitely grateful for this moment. It seemed crazy to her that they were walking through the streets of the marina that were so every day for her, but that for him were a wonderful novelty.

Laila found this reality to be in contrast to that of a few weeks ago when, overwhelmed with helplessness, they thought they would never see each other again and that what started at an airport would be just a nice memory of one more trip.

She couldn't help but remember those first conversations with him, after having revealed her secret first to her older sister, her greatest accomplice in all this, and then to her mother.

Her mind traveled without a ticket seven months back, to mid-September when, after being heartbroken to leave her grandmother

Jamila and grandfather Omar, she returned home with her parents, Samia, Karim, and her nephews.

It was strange to think of Dubai as home after having been in Raouche. Now she was just another tourist on those wide streets of the waterfront that guarded the Beirut Sea. Logically, the return and the mixture of emotions that she was experiencing, for the first time, left her with a state of mind that she hardly knew how to recognize and even less how to address. Having Elias, at least through her cell phone, was a relief.

After telling him about how strange she felt returning home after her time in the land where she was born and spent her early years, Elias proposed an activity to lift her spirits. Creativity would be an important ally if they wanted to shorten the distance and feel close to each other, despite being considerably far away.

The activity was simple but fun. Laila had to choose a dish from Lebanese traditional cuisine, buy the ingredients, and share that list of ingredients with Elias. Then they would agree on a day and time, and both would cook the same dish by video call. Laila immediately felt excited about the virtual plan and without thinking or meditating too much her mind chose for her: *Knafeh*!

Elias was surprised, as he had never tried it, and he was excited about the idea of preparing and eating something new. She started by sending him several voice notes in which she explained the pronunciation of this word, which, like many in the language, was not pronounced as it was read. Once this level was overcome, she shared the recipe and the ingredients.

"I think you'll be able to get everything there without a problem," she commented, and when Elias checked the shopping list, he knew it would be an easier task than he imagined. He could also imagine the combination of cheese, pistachios, syrup, and noodles and felt his salivary glands soak his mouth. Sweets were his weakest point.

During his visit to the market, he had fun selecting ingredients, taking pictures with his cell phone, and seeking the approval of the chef who was waiting for him for a culinary date on the other side of the world.

"Can you see me?" She asked, while accommodating her cellphone in the kitchen's countertop.

"I see you." Elias said as a huge smile took over his face.

"I want you to meet Dalida. My mother. As much as I want to pretend, I know how to cook *Knafeh*, my mom is the expert." Laila commented, her voice cracking with laughter.

Dalida waved and offered her daughter's new friend a warm smile. The culinary adventure began, and it felt unreal to him to be cooking with his potential girlfriend and her potential mother-in-law.

The help of technology and the way everything seemed to flow between them made the distances disappear. As if in an alternate universe, Elias and Laila came together to cook in the same physical and temporal space.

Maybe they met in Laila's family's luxurious villa in Dubai to prepare *Knafeh* or, perhaps, they arranged to meet at Elias' parents' house to make rice pudding that would flood the house with that warm and sweet smell that reminded him of his childhood.

It didn't matter if it was the exotic cheese with noodles and syrup or if it was that rich rice pudding with milk, sugar, and cinnamon, for both of them, each dish represented exactly the same thing: childhood, home, mother's love, and a feeling of knowing that with a bite everything would be fine and that even the ugliest of problems would be driven away by the smell emanating from the oven.

After dirtying the kitchens, preheating the oven, greasing, flouring, and chopping, the *Knafeh* was ready. Both Elias' and Laila's.

"Well... It's moment of truth! Let's taste it!" She said, opening the invitation to her virtual diner, who, at times, seemed to her to be sitting on one of the high stools in her kitchen.

Elias cut a piece and took it to his mouth. It was an explosion of flavors, the sweet mixed with the slightly salty cheese, the delicate texture of the phyllo pastry noodles felt like butter melting on his tongue, and the characteristic flavor of the pistachios added a unique touch to the dessert.

No words were needed; his face said it all. His eyes closed, and his mouth wouldn't stop; he wanted to savor it carefully.

"Hey, this is delicious. Please tell your mom thank you so much for the cooking class and let her know that I'm going to make this dessert for my parents when I see them this weekend."

"I'm glad you liked it," she said with a smile as she turned to let Dalida know her friend's message.

Before saying goodbye, Elias gave a new surprise.

"If you liked this plan, I have a proposal for the weekend... Do you like movies? Like... Classic movies."

Excitement crackled in the air as Saturday arrived, bringing with it the virtual movie night Elias had planned for Laila. They'd discovered a shared love for the classics of Hollywood's golden age, and their choice for the evening was a movie that had been high on both of their watchlists for a long time: *Casablanca*.

While Elias had to start his virtual movie day at one in the afternoon, Laila had to wait almost until midnight. She laughingly told her Mexican friend that she had taken a short nap to power through the wait since the movie they both chose was almost two hours long. Elias couldn't help but laugh and joke, making references to contemporary movies that lasted much longer than the classic set in Morocco.

"The Hateful Eight by Tarantino is over three hours long."

"True," she replied, "but movies of the golden age used to have a much slower pace."

"Okay, I'm going to send you a link," he said through the video call. A practice that, between them, was becoming increasingly normalized.

Elias had done some research prior to the meeting. He'd been looking for activities for friends, family, or couples in long-distance relationships. He found an application that synchronized the screens and allowed two or more viewers to watch the same series or movie at the same time.

Laila was excited. Not only was she thrilled to finally tick this movie off her list, but she also loved to see that her new acquaintance was making an effort to spend quality time "together." And that's how he felt too. If he had to describe these encounters, he would have surely written the word together without having to frame it within quotation marks.

Elias could almost feel her chopping pistachios in the kitchen of her house, asking him where she kept the special "chef" knives or preparing popcorn to watch a movie together in the living room of his apartment.

He had no doubt that if he felt this connection so intensely, she was surely experiencing something very similar.

And the truth is, even though they were not physically together, their souls or some spiritual aspect of both had been joined by the invisible red thread since that encounter planned by fortune. Good fortune. This spiritual bond, forged in the crucible of that providential encounter, resonated in every choice they made, in every experience they lived separately but that, in some way, were intertwined with the other's story. As if each step they took resonated in the other's heart.

It could be said that their souls were like travelers in a parallel universe, sharing an ethereal space where physical limitations were irrelevant. Perhaps, within the essence of this spiritual bond, they found solace in the certainty that, although their bodies were separated, their souls never ceased to walk together on the paths of life. Like two stars, distant in the firmament yet sharing the same sky, they illuminated each other in the darkness of the night. Thus, the invisible red thread that bound them became the eternal testimony of a connection that transcended the limitations of the tangible world.

"Ready? Can I press play?" Laila asked, pulling Elias out of the whirlwind of his thoughts.

An hour and forty-two minutes later, Laila felt warm tears running down her cheeks. She couldn't help but wonder if that final scene, depicting a love that remained a promise despite the miles that would separate them, had moved Elias as deeply as it had moved her.

Suddenly, she noticed her cell phone screen light up and hurried to read the message, knowing perfectly well who the sender was.

Elias:

Hey Lai, I don't know if we'll ever have our Paris, but we'll always have Dubai... Dubai Airport.

Laila <3:

The truth is, we need to have a serious conversation. I'm not like the girls you're used to date.

The message left Elias frozen. On one hand, he loved knowing and confirming that she saw this as more than just a virtual friendship keeping his hope of becoming something more alive. But, due to his Arab heritage, he could sense the implications and the formality he would have to adhere to, without any certainty of a future. The thought felt like an abyss in the center of his chest, one he wasn't ready to jump into. Not yet.

Days passed, and communication shifted from intense and constant to sporadic and spaced-out messages. Something had changed that night, a secret evident to both Laila and Elias, known only to Humphrey Bogart and Ingrid Bergman, yet chosen to be ignored.

A few more days passed, and as Elias drove late one night through the streets of downtown Saltillo, a song began to play that immediately reminded him of her. Before rationality kicked in, he grabbed his phone, recorded a video of his music player screen, and sent it across the world. They had become masters of each other's routines over the previous days of constant conversation and schedule coordination. They knew when each other woke up, worked, ate, exercised, and went to bed.

Elias sent the message at eleven at night, and Laila received it at nine in the morning, already starting her day, or as he jokingly told her, coming from the future. Suddenly, Elias's phone began to ring. It was a message from her.

Laila <3

Hey Elias, what are you doing awake?

Elias_

Ugh, hey. Couldn't sleep because of insomnia, so I went for a walk. Guilt's eating me alive

Laila <3_

Guilty? What about?

Elias_

I never replied to your message and things have felt distant. My bad.

Laila <3_

Well, do you want to reply to me now?

Elias took advantage of the moment and the inspiring background music to tell her that he knew she was not like the other women he knew. And that made her special, but that naturally the sudden commitment made him feel anxious.

Elias_

But Lai, now that I've overcome my anxiety and realized that I've missed you during these days of being "distant", I'd rather jump into the void with everything to

lose, but also everything to
gain.

Laila <3_

I feel like I was starting to
enjoy our virtual plans.

Elias_

We were already on our
second formal date.

Laila <3_

Very funny. To be honest, I
did find it very funny
Hahaha.

Elias_

I propose something, let me
plan the third date. I promise
not to disappoint.

Laila <3_

Perfect. I accept the
invitation. Hey, after all,

we've had two dates and
you haven't had to meet my
dad yet.

Elias_

Now you're the funny one.

Days passed and Laila was waiting in anticipation, knowing that Elias had promised to surprise her. So, she preferred to always be available and at home so she could be ready when the time came for the long-awaited third virtual date. It was during one of those days of waiting when she found a special invitation in her email.

From: <eliasmram@gmail.com>
Reply-To: <eliasmram@gmail.com>
To: laila1995nov@gmail.com
Date: Oct 24, 2022, 7:14 PM
Subject: Lunch in Dubai, Dinner in Saltillo (It's a Date!)

My dearest Laila,

Get ready for something special! You and your sister Samia are invited to a fancy lunch (all expenses paid!), while 'I'll be having dinner back in Saltillo. But don't worry, we can chat during the event! Just bring your phone.

Your sister, Samia, will fill you in on all the details soon. The location is a surprise, so get ready for anything!

I can't wait for Saturday!

Best,

Elias

A few hours later, Samia called Laila and without revealing too many details, asked her to leave a space in her schedule for the following Saturday. She only had to tell her parents that she was going to lunch with her sister, so the outing would not be a problem. She was happy and couldn't stop smiling since she received that email. This was the third date and she couldn't wait for Saturday.

Chapter Four

Surprise!

"I crossed oceans of time to find you."
Dracula by Bram Stoker

Samia and Laila arrived at a place they both knew had delicious food. In fact, it was one of their family's favorite restaurants when they wanted to eat something different. Laila realized her older sister was definitely in on this surprise.

"How did Elias get Samia's contact?" she thought as she settled into her seat. The sisters had arrived that Saturday for their reservation at the Swiss Butter restaurant at the Novotel Al Barsha Hotel. This place mainly offered cuts of meat, chicken, and salmon, all served with a delicious sauce that Laila and every member of her large family loved.

Thanks to a lucky coincidence, there was also a branch in Lebanon, and when they traveled to visit their maternal grandparents in their homeland, they also used to enjoy this place that promised to indulge their palates.

The time difference meant that Samia and Elias had to agree on a lunch for them at twelve noon, while in Saltillo, he would have a late dinner. The older sister, Elias's new partner-in-crime, wanted to impress Laila with a visit to Swiss Butter. She knew that, in addition to delicious food, this place served one of her sister's favorite desserts: French toast with ice cream (known as *pain perdu* on the other side of the world).

The restaurant's famous *pain perdu* was served in a hot casserole. A piece of fluffy bread, like a cloud, topped with a scoop of butter ice cream and a caramel sauce that gave the perfect touch to that delight. But, although Laila could taste the dessert from the moment she arrived, she knew that other dishes would come first.

The order arrived at the table: salmon, served with that sauce that made this place very special, French fries, salad, bread, and, the best part, a little bit of *sumac*. When she saw the table filled with appetizing food, she took her cell phone, took a picture and shared it with Elias, thanking him for this moment and for the banquet.

Elias received the message while he was taking a pizza out of the box to heat it up in his home oven. He had stopped by an Italian restaurant called MM Pizzas that was quite popular in Saltillo. This was one of his favorite places in his city, but since he saw it complicated to eat there and be able to coincide with Laila and Samia due to the schedule, he made an order to take away well in advance.

When he saw the photo, Elias craved what Laila and her sister were having for lunch. He had ordered his favorite pizza, the one he always ordered at this place.

Elias _

Hey Lai, there's no doubt. If I were in Dubai, eating with you... I would steal your plate. Let's see if you can guess what I just ordered.

Laila <3_

Hey, there's no doubt that I wouldn't let you try one single bite. Hahahaha. Can you give me a hint?

Elias _

I picked up food at a place I love that fuses Mexican and Italian cuisine.

Laila <3_

A... pizza?

Elias _

You guessed it! And you also
brought me luck, because
the oven just went off and
it's ready.

Elias snapped a picture of his delicious-looking pizza. He even filmed a short video showing how he'd set the table at home, trying to recreate the restaurant's ambiance for his virtual dinner. Laila couldn't help but comment on his tempting meal: thin crust piled high with olives, feta cheese, and sun-dried tomatoes. Behind the pizza, she noticed a bottle of Tabasco sauce and dried *peperoncino* seeds. She understood that her Mexican friend loved spicy food.

Both Elias and Laila made a playful promise. "Someday," he'd take her to MM Pizzas for a feast amidst the seasonal decor, and she'd return the favor by treating him to *pain perdu* at the Swiss Butter in Beirut.

Without wasting a beat, Laila searched online for the restaurant Elias mentioned, piecing together a mental image. On the other side of the globe, her virtual dinner companion was doing the same. Lost in a daydream, she barely registered her sister's conversation fading. She pictured herself in that warm, inviting space —brick walls, exposed bulbs overhead— a cozy haven in the heart of Elias's city.

In that moment, the physical distance between them seemed to melt away, replaced by the magic of their imaginations. Their creative minds became accomplices, defying the limitations of geography. Though separated by kilometers, they found solace in the idea that their thoughts could converge, as if tangible reality dissolved under the power of their shared dreams. It was like exploring a realm where the concrete world blurred at the edges, and their souls could dance together and free inside an ethereal space, unbound by the earthly constraints of physics.

The red thread that connected them felt like more than a metaphor; it was an invisible force that transcended logic, guiding their hearts towards a perfect harmony. Their souls, intertwined in an embrace, found comfort in this undeniable connection that weathered any storm. It was as if their very essences had forged a timeless pact, vowing to remain connected regardless of external circumstances.

This powerful bond wasn't just a promise of future closeness, but an affirmation that their destinies were intricately linked. Like two magnets drawn together with irresistible force, their paths seemed destined to converge. The metaphor of being positioned at opposite corners of the same electrical current resonated deeply, illustrating how, despite their seeming polarities, their life forces shared a common current, destined to merge in a cosmic union.

While the physical distance remained, their unwavering connection acted as a powerful magnet, bridging the gap and forging a bond that transcended earthly boundaries. In this shared universe of thoughts and desires, separation became merely a prelude to their inevitable reunion.

That day, when Laila returned home to her parents' house after spending an incredible evening with Elias and her sister Samia, she took her cell phone and wrote a heartfelt thank you message. It was a response to the sudden and furtive invitation she had received from Elias days ago.

From: <laila1995nov@gmail.com>
Reply to: <laila1995nov@gmail.com>
To: eliasmram@gmail.com
Date: Oct 29, 2022, 6:00 PM
Subject: Thank you for everything! Shukran

Dear Mr. Elias.

I wanted to thank you for today's date. I really enjoyed the food, the company, learning about how much you enjoy spicy food, and, above all, I am left with the idea of one day getting to know Saltillo and showing you Dubai and Raouche.

I have good news for you. I wanted to tell you that next week, we won't have to juggle to communicate despite the time difference. My sister asked me during lunch to accompany her to New York. Her husband has a business trip and invited us to spend a few days. I said yes, but with the idea of being able to be physically a little closer to you. For 5 days (from November 24 to 28) we will be almost in the same time zone.

I hope that when you wake up in a few hours you have a nice day.

Warm regards,
Laila.

The notification sound of Laila's email woke Elias from his sleep. It was unusual; he was a heavy sleeper and rarely bothered by small noises. With heavy eyes, he reached for his phone on the nightstand. Seeing Laila's email address on the screen jolted him awake. He sat up, his heart pounding as he started to read the message. A smile spread across his face as he read her opening words, but by the time he finished, his heart was racing.

"New York?" he thought, rereading the message to confirm he hadn't misread. How could this be possible? Elias stumbled out of bed and fumbled for his calendar in the darkness. It was a small brown leather notebook, a gift from his mother on his last birthday. "So you can write down all your big goals and see how they come true," mom said, handing it to him wrapped in delicate paper at their family dinner. His mother had a talent for crafts.

He found the calendar on a chair and flipped through the pages to November. There, in his own handwriting, was the entry he was looking for:

MON	TUE	WED	THUR	FRI	SAT	SUN
21	22	23	24	25	26	27
Trio to NYC	Trio to NYC	Trip to NYC	Trip to NYC			

Just a month ago, shortly after starting his new job at the Universidad del Valle de México, the dean of his faculty had requested his presence at a major conference in Manhattan during the last days of November. It was a forum hosted by the Mexico-United States Chamber of Commerce.

Leaving the dean's office, Elias had felt a surge of excitement. This was a fantastic opportunity! While most of his thoughts at that time were occupied by Laila, the mysterious girl he'd met at the airport, this professional development felt like a personal win as well.

Back in the dark room, a new thought struck Elias. "I'll be in New York for a day with Laila!" he realized. On Thursday, November 24th, they'd be in the same city, at the same time. The thought sent a wave of nervous excitement through him. It was only 4:12 AM, but sleep seemed to have vanished entirely. A whirlwind of questions and possibilities flooded his mind.

Should he confide in Samia, who was also going on the trip and had already been a trusted confidante? He liked her and they communicated easily. Or should he maintain the element of surprise and simply show up in New York, hoping to see her? He was apprehensive about the idea of seeing her being misconstrued as overstepping or disrespectful. Laila had made it clear she wasn't like other girls, and although her family practiced a moderate form of Islam, she seemed to hold some traditional values.

Elias had been researching about *halal* love on social media —a concept of lawful love achieved through marriage and a formal request to the *wali* (guardian) of the girl's hand. But being in the same city and not being able to see each other also seemed absurd to him. He decided he wouldn't say anything and that, just as their meeting and friendship had been guided by destiny, he would wait until he was in the city that never sleeps to make a decision on the matter. If he was lucky, he might even receive a sign of serendipity.

Chapter Five

Hell's Kitchen

"Marry someone who looks at you as if you were magic."
Frida Kahlo

Elias exited the airport and took a taxi, giving the driver the address of his rented apartment. It was Monday and he was eager to get settled so he could work on his presentation for the next day.

The yellow cab dropped him off at a modern, light-brick building. He'd meticulously written down the address in his planner: 315 W 5th St., New York. He preferred to have everything documented. He was in Hell's Kitchen, near the southern entrance of Central Park. He had chosen a comfortable but simple location close to the forum site.

He dropped his suitcase, took out his gray laptop, and started working on his presentation, which he had already made significant progress on. Sitting in a brownish, semi-leather chair, the hours slipped by. He glanced out the window and realized it was already dark. Saving his work, he grabbed the coat he'd traveled with and headed out for a walk around the neighborhood. His stomach was urgently demanding attention.

Exiting the building, he noticed the cool air. Saltillo had definitely been colder. He was thankful this trip coincided with New York's pleasant autumn weather. The oppressive summer heat was gone, and the snowy chills of winter hadn't arrived yet. The neighborhood buzzed with life. Pedestrians chatted, shop lights glowed, music drifted by, cars honked, and sirens wailed —the city's unique soundscape.

Elias walked several blocks in a straight line, passing countless traffic lights. He recalled his first trip to the "Big Apple" with friends. That experience had been entirely different. They'd embarked on a whirlwind tour, hitting all the tourist spots: museums, the Statue of Liberty, the Wall Street Bull, the Met steps, the Coney Island amusement park rides, zoos, and endless subway journeys.

The aroma emanating from a street food cart made him stop and consider his dinner options. Lost in his thoughts, he hadn't realized he'd been walking for almost forty minutes. He was just a few steps away from the iconic Chelsea Market's brick facade. He remembered one of his favorite noodle spots —Very Fresh Noodles— was located inside.

He walked through the market's many options until he spotted the familiar sight: a light wood bar bordering a kitchen with spotless white tiles and a glass partition separating cooks from diners. The place was simple, not fancy, but as often happens in the city, delicious food didn't require a posh atmosphere.

Looking at the menu, he made his choice: a classic ramen with freshly made noodles, famous in the city for their near three-meter length. The noodles arrived surprisingly quickly, served in a bowl over a dark broth, with chives and bok choy, the popular Chinese cabbage. The hungry traveler devoured the food, thoroughly satisfied. He paid the bill, left a good tip, and rose from his seat to head back to his rented apartment.

The day of the forum arrived, and nerves gnawed at Elias throughout his presentation. However, he received congratulations from all his colleagues afterward. Among those present was Daniela, a young woman working at the Mexican embassy in New York who'd been invited to the event. Elias couldn't help but notice Daniela's persistent gaze, which made him feel uncomfortable. With Laila, there were no guarantees, yet his attraction to her was so strong that even the thought of "flirting" with Daniela felt unthinkable.

Something had shifted within him. He pondered how powerful it was that this girl from a faraway land, whom he was just getting to know, could make him feel this way. That immature, selfish, and impulsive version of himself seemed a distant memory.

"Laila makes me want to be a better man in every way," he thought. "I have to find a way to see her."

Elias' plan was to surprise Laila on Thursday, November 24th, their only day in the same city. However, a complication arose: on that day, he couldn't reach either Laila or Samia. Time was running out. A driver would pick him up at 1:00 PM to take him to the New Jersey airport. It was already 10:00 AM.

Elias began packing and getting everything ready, so that as soon as he heard from her, or from her sister, he could move quickly. He needed to see her, even if it was just for five minutes.

Time seemed indifferent to love's urgency that Thursday, relentlessly ticking forward. Time, that fickle friend, toyed with lovers, granting them moments that felt like forever and snatching away their most precious fragments in a blink of an eye.

Each tick-tock resonated with a strange contrast. While lost in moments of joy, the seconds seemed to shorten, as if they enjoyed the pleasure of accompanying his happiness bit by bit. However, when the shadow of sadness loomed, time adopted an achingly slow pace, as if it wanted to hold back every tear and sigh every sorrow.

The same measure that marked the minutes became an unhelpful partner for Elias' emotions, running a frantic sprint that morning. The minutes, usually elastic and flexible, now seemed more like athletes in a desperate race. The speed with which time was consumed felt as if fate itself was determined to test the strength of love.

Time, that wily conjurer, cast its spell to defy logic and remind Elias that every second was a precious jewel that deserved to be admired, however fleetingly, in the symphony of his love.

"Ping," the phone rang, and with that sound, Elias' stomach felt hollow. AS if the entire universe could fit inside that bodily cavity. "Could it be them?" he wondered. Grabbing his phone, the device that connected him to her daily, he saw it was the driver. He was waiting for him on the street in front of the building.

Defeated, Elias picked up his suitcases and felt his eyes well up with tears. He roughly ran his hand across his face, interrupting the flow and wiping away any trace of them. He closed the apartment door, entered a code, and left the keys inside the key safe.

He took the elevator down and upon reaching the building lobby, he said goodbye to the friendly Dominican man who had greeted him and seen him off during his stay. The man helped him open the heavy glass door leading to the street and took one of his suitcases to make things easier for him. Elias took out his wallet and took out some bills to thank him for his hospitality with a tip. He looked around, as if wanting to absorb the city in one last look.

Amid the chaotic and disorderly bustle of the great city of New York, her presence emerged. It was Laila, accompanied by her sister and niece. Elias, immersed in the chaos of the city, found himself suddenly paralyzed, his eyes fixed on Laila's figure. A disturbing question took hold of his mind: was his tired mind playing tricks on him, or was reality manifesting itself before him in a surprising way? Unable to resist the need to corroborate what he was seeing, he directed a question to the doorman in the hope that he would share his peculiar vision.

"Can you see those three girls standing on the street in front of us?" Elias asked, hoping he wasn't alone in this perception. The doorman, without hesitation, nodded and complimented how beautiful the three women were.

The doorman's comment unleashed a torrent of emotions in Elias, from anger to the urge to snatch the tip back at that very moment. However, the disconcerting paralysis took hold of him, as if an invisible cable had been disconnected, leaving his reason in a confusing emptiness.

In a desperate attempt to break the silence, Elias tried to shout at Laila, but an invisible force prevented him from coordinating his body with his thoughts. "LAILA!" his internal scream resounded, though barely a whisper escaped his lips.

He tried again, this time trying to imprint more force, but shyness still marked his voice. "Laila!" he shouted, although she seemed to barely perceive the faint call. She turned her head, but her eyes did not meet Elias's.

In an unexpected twist of fate, Laila headed towards a yellow taxi waiting for them, where Samia and Amira eagerly awaited to venture into the shops of the Big Apple. The taxi slowly drove away, leaving Elias behind, powerless and with his gaze lost in the distance.

Defeated, he entered his own taxi, maintaining a heavy silence throughout the journey. Inside the vehicle, an internal debate erupted, with accusatory thoughts resonating in his mind: "Why didn't you do anything?", "You should have shouted louder", "What a coward!", "When will you have another chance to see her?".

Doubts and reproaches intertwined, weaving a complicated web of anguish around Elias's heart, while the city continued with its frenetic pace, as if caring little about the defeat of one of its visitors.

As the taxi navigated through the bustling streets, Elias couldn't help but feel a sense of regret washing over him. He replayed the moment in his mind, wishing he had summoned the courage to express his feelings more boldly. The opportunity had slipped through his fingers, leaving him grappling with what-ifs and missed chances.

Yet amidst the turmoil of his thoughts, a glimmer of hope flickered. Perhaps this wasn't the end of their story. Maybe fate would intervene once again, granting him another chance encounter with Laila. With this thought in mind, Elias vowed to seize any future opportunities that came his way, determined not to let fear hold him back.

As the taxi turned a corner, Elias caught a glimpse of the city skyline, illuminated by the glow of daylight and towering skyscrapers. In that moment, he felt a surge of determination coursing through him.

Whatever the future held, he would face it head-on, ready to pursue his heart's desires without hesitation.

Chapter Six

City Flowers

"Many eyes go through the meadow,

but few see the flowers in it."

Ralph Waldo Emerson

Frustrated by his inability to act at the crucial moment, Elias found himself immersed in a dark melancholy that spread like a shadow over his days. He took his cell phone and reached out in a desperate attempt to communicate with Laila, sharing with her the bitterness of having missed the opportunity to have her close. The return to the New Jersey airport became a torturous journey, marked by the feeling of being trapped in a void, where time and space lost their usual meaning and the simple act of breathing became more complicated.

Elias _

I can't believe it. I just saw you.
You were getting into a taxi in
Hell's Kitchen, with Samia and
Amira.

The geographical distance between Mexico and Dubai became insignificant compared to the emotional gap that separated Elias from Laila. Despite the days that passed since that ephemeral encounter in New York, the horrible feeling of having let a valuable opportunity slip away persisted in his mind. The tormenting "what if..." became a constant echo that haunted him even in his dreams, feeding an uncertainty that turned into a ghost, harassing him day and night.

The mirror of time reflected not only his face, but also his deep sadness. The shadow of what could have been projected onto his thoughts, transforming his reflections into a playful dance with the uncertainty of a future that would never materialize.

Tormented by the idea of an encounter that would never exist in this life, Elias plunged into speculation about alternate universes, imagining a version of himself, but braver and capable of facing that paralyzing reality. "What would have become of me if I had made another decision, taken another path? I would have been happy, I would have achieved my dreams, I would have been different," he thought.

Possible scenarios flashed through his mind like a movie. He saw vivid images of her being happy to see him, others where she remained silent, he envisioned scenes of rejection and from there he went to the other extreme: ecstasy, happiness, overflowing love. Everything was possible and everything was possible at that moment on that street in Hell's Kitchen.

Swept up in a whirlwind of thoughts, Elias had an idea. It was Sunday, so he jumped out of bed where he had spent the last hours of the day. He sat at his desk, opened his laptop and started typing away. It seemed that he was becoming a master at keeping the flame of love alive, while being thousands and thousands of miles away from her.

He found a flower shop that offered its services in the Middle East and knowing that he was just a few steps away from successfully fulfilling his goal for that Sunday, he found the perfect bouquet: lisianthus, mini roses in pastel pink and white tones and eucalyptus.

He wrote Laila's address, added details to the personalized note and pressed the button that completed the purchase. The thrill of this small act was enough to shake him out of the lethargy that those days in New York had left him, after an encounter that never was.

After feeling so close, yet so far, this gesture brought him closer to her again. Elias searched his memory bank, where he stored phrases from books, movies, series and lecturers that had marked him. Then he remembered a phrase by Françoise Sagan about love and madness that he liked very much. He decided to share it with Laila and asked that it be written on the note that would accompany his flowers.

"I have loved to the point of madness; and what they call madness, to me, is the only sane way to love".

Françoise Sagan

Laila, I am sending you these flowers to let you know that I am still thinking of you. I hope you like them.

With all my love,

Elías

The flowers were not only a tangible gift, but also a symbol of hope, a hopeful sign that despite the distance, their relationship continued and that the future held the promise of many shared joys. These flowers became a bond that connected their hearts despite the distance, a living reminder that love, like flowers, can bloom and thrive even in distant and seemingly barren lands.

Days later, in a corner of Dubai, Laila received the package with the beautiful flowers that Elias had sent her from Mexico. The bouquet was a symphony of colors and fragrances that filled the room where she placed them with excitement and anticipation. Taking the delicate arrangement in her hands, a smile spread across her face as she read the personalized note that accompanied the gift.

Inspired by Elias' gesture and chivalry, she took a beautiful piece of opaline paper with her initials embossed in a fine gold color. She chose a purple pen and began to write a letter in her own handwriting. When she finished, she took a picture of it and shared it with Elias.

In the message that accompanied the letter, Laila wrote:

Laila <3 _

Just as you sent me flowers,

I wanted to write you a letter.

I'm sending it to you via WhatsApp

so it doesn't take an eternity to arrive.

Dearest Elías,

These flowers arrived like a breath of fresh air to my day. Their beauty is as radiant as the love we share, and their fragrance feels like a hug from a distance, you have reminded me that even though we are separated by miles, the miles between us can't waken our connection.

The quote from Françoise Sagan that you chose has touched my heart. In each petal I find the promise of a love that defies distances and overcomes any obstacle. Thank you for this beautiful and meaningful gesture. You have put a smile back on my face and filled my day with light and color.

I look forward to the moment when we can meet again in person, but in the meantime, these flowers become a tangible reminder of our love that grows like these beautiful flowers

With all my love,

Laila

Chapter Seven

The Scent of a New City

"If you like someone for their physique, it's not love, it's desire. If you like them for their intelligence, it's not love, it's admiration. If you like them for their wealth, it's not love, it's interest. But if you don't know why you like them... Then, that is love."

Arabic proverb

Elias was completely consumed by a sense of anxiety that far exceeded the expectations he had calculated in his rational mind.

As "the moment" approached, the magnitude of his nervousness reached unexpected levels. Despite his efforts to cling to logic, he found it difficult to understand that in the intricate matters of the heart and feelings, the authority of reason was scarce, almost non-existent. The anticipation of the days and events to come added an additional layer to his anxiety, orchestrating a disorderly symphony of emotions that resisted submitting to the baton of logic, which Elias valued so much in other aspects of his life. He didn't like feeling that, at times, he could lose control of what would happen in the future.

He felt the force of the plane as it made contact with the concrete runway. The pressure of the landing added to the nerves that had been growing in his stomach. For minutes, he remained paralyzed in his seat. He felt that even though his brain was sending the command to stand up, his legs and arms were clinging to the metal seat of the plane. Then an inner voice appeared to help clear away his fears: "You didn't travel more than thirteen thousand kilometers to stay here sitting down. Don't let what happened in New York happen again."

The thought was enough for his body to spring into action. He stood up, took his hand luggage and walked down the narrow aisle. He noticed that by the time he left, almost all the passengers had left the aircraft.

He knew that each step brought him closer to that moment he had dreamed of, but which also terrified him and which he had invited anxiety to keep him company the last few days. Welcome to Dubai, he read on an advertisement inside the airport. The same place where, eight months ago, the adventure, the coincidence and the magic of the chance encounter that brought them together had begun. He could only wonder if this story... his story, Laila's, theirs, would have a happy ending.

After the immigration procedures, which felt like an eternity, he went outside and got into a taxi. It was April and the temperatures had started to rise. He rolled down the car window and felt the warm air lightly hit his face. The smells captivated him and, strangely, made him feel at home.

The air in this faraway city smelled like a delicious mixture of cumin, cardamom, saffron and nutmeg. The pungent stench of car fumes permeated the air to dull any pleasant aroma. Suddenly, notes of a scent of incense, sea, tea and coffee appeared... Of her. How could it be possible if, until now, he had not been able to smell her? He knew that it would not be immediate either to get to know her smell, as he understood that he had to keep his distance out of respect.

There was something about those aromas that reminded him of something familiar, warm and known. He felt at home, without being there. Unlike the previous trip, he was no longer a tourist. Now he felt like he belonged. Elias had booked a room at the Four Points by Sheraton in the city center. He didn't know if it was close or far from Laila's house, but at least he knew they were in the same place and breathing the same air, and that, that night for the first time, they would sleep wrapped in the light of the same moonlit sky.

The taxi ride lasted just over 15 minutes. He entered the hotel through the glass revolving doors and once he checked in, he went up to the fourth floor to find his room. He walked down a long hallway until he found the door he was looking for. Room 5. He inserted the magnetic key and turned the iron doorknob that felt cold against the skin of his hand. Upon entering, he found a simple room, decorated with warm colors and a huge, comfortable-looking bed in the middle of the room.

He left his bags aside and walked straight to the windows. He pulled back the curtains of light white fabric and noticed that the views were not that impressive. Tall buildings, possibly other hotels and their swimming pools. Seeing the clock in the room, Elias realized that it was nine at night. He undressed and as he was, he fell asleep on that bed.

Elias woke up with the sun's rays warming his face. He had forgotten to close the curtains of the room he had rented for a few days. He looked again at the electric clock in the room: seven in the morning. He stretched, got rid of the sheets and walked to the bathroom. He took a hot shower and came out of the bathroom feeling like new. He got dressed and took his cell phone. The nerves returned.

Then he knew it was time to notify Samia of his arrival in the city and continue with the plan as they had agreed. This time the surprise was not for Laila, but for her parents, Hassan and Dalida.

After breakfast, Samia picked up Elias at the hotel. She was accompanied by her husband Karim. That morning everything was so new that Elias, despite having an infinite number of options for breakfast, barely ate a piece of toast with butter and some jam. He ordered coffee, but only took a few sips. The nerves occupied a real and important space in his stomach.

Karim drove while Samia, attentively, tried to make conversation with Elias. It was possible that they would end up being family and, besides, her sister had entrusted her with the mission of making him feel comfortable. The conversation became pleasant and natural, and Elias didn't notice the thirty minutes that had passed inside the car, traveling a practically straight path from his hotel to a place called Al Furjan.

At some point on the way, he turned to the right and saw the famous Jumeirah Palm through the car window. An artificial island, in the shape of a palm tree, that housed luxury hotels, residential towers, restaurants, beach clubs, swimming pools and nightclubs. Elias had not visited Dubai on his previous trip, he had only made a stopover at the airport, so these views were dazzling him.

After the straight drive, Karim turned right. They entered a residential area of what Elias identified as villas. Everything looked very organized and clean. The cream-colored buildings were surrounded by perfectly pruned shrubs and palm trees, very typical of the area.

"Very nice, right?" asked Samia with a tone of pride in her voice.

"It's beautiful."

"Not to brag, but this is one of the residential complexes that Dad helped develop. He's an architect. But surely Laila already told you about him."

"If Samia knew," Elias thought, and kept his thoughts to himself. He remembered that as soon as Laila told him about what her father did and some of the projects he had worked on as an architect in Dubai, he ran to the internet search engine to look for all the information possible. Elias also thought that this residential area seemed very beautiful to him. Much more than what he had seen in photos.

The architecture of each small house had a very characteristic Middle Eastern style, however, the type of complex seemed quite suburban and contemporary to him.

The car stopped and the nerves intensified.

"Welcome," said Karim with a smile and genuine kindness.

"Thank you very much! And thanks for the ride" replied Elias, thinking that this man would very possibly become his family in the next few months.

As he entered the house through a wide gate, Elias immediately recognized the intoxicating smell of nuts that basmati rice has. The aroma came from a room to his right that must have been the kitchen. Samia and Karim led him to a central living room, decorated with soft cream-colored sofas. The neutrality of the furniture was interrupted by the colors of the rugs and the heavy floral print curtains.

From the huge windows he could see a patio with a swimming pool, barbecue and a cozy gazebo. Elias was fascinated, because, immediately, he could give a real context to what he had imagined of Laila and her life kilometers away from his. He could imagine her there, with her family, in dozens of events and celebrations. Enjoying the pool with her three nephews or having breakfast outdoors, on a weekend, with her parents. The thoughts he had about her became more vivid.

"Hello Elias. Nice to meet you" said a husky female voice that suddenly entered the room where Elias, Karim and Samia were waiting. Elias noticed that it was Dalida, Laila's mother. "Well, although we have already met. We cooked a delicious..."

"*Knafeh*," said Elias smiling and trying his best with the pronunciation.

When he saw her, he found a short lady. She also wore a *hijab*; her skin was white and very well preserved. She had green eyes like two olives, and thick, very blonde eyebrows. She wore glasses to see, with a modern, rounded and bright pink frame. The smell of her perfume filled the room. It was sweet, intoxicating, delicious. It was a very "motherly" aroma.

The kindness of her gaze had made him feel more comfortable. But the most complex part of the day still remained: to meet Hassan, the father, and, of course, to see her again.

A torrent of anxious thoughts flooded his mind, Elias wondered if after making all this effort and crossing seas to see her, he would still feel the same when they were face to face. Or at least in the same room, accompanied by all the chaperones necessary.

Then the invasion of thoughts was interrupted by the patriarch. Hassan, now was the protagonist of the love story of Laila and Elias. With a simple "no", he could become the villain and put an end to the romantic novel that was just beginning to write its first pages.

"Good morning, Elias! And welcome to my home," said Hassan as he approached his potential new son-in-law to shake his hand firmly. "My wife has prepared us a delicious *biryani*. Do you eat seafood?"

Elias managed to nod, as the awkwardness generated by his nerves momentarily blocked the flow of his words.

Fortunately, Dalida interrupted the uncomfortable silence. "Elias, *biryani* is a very popular dish here in Dubai. I learned how to prepare it after eating it a lot in some local restaurants. It is traditionally prepared to welcome a special guest or to celebrate an occasion."

"Mom makes it delicious," Samia added. "It's basically the only point where India and Pakistan agree. Because after these countries separated in the forties, they had nothing in common but biryani."

"Thank you, daughter, for reminding us of the historical side of this dish," Hassan said with a proud smile.

That night in his hotel, after tasting the exquisite dish and trying to review the day full of emotions, Elias would search his cell phone for more information about *biryani*. He would learn that it is made by frying cubes of fish, shrimp and squid. After draining, they are placed in clay pots. They are covered with a layer of basmati rice, numerous spices, water are added and everything is sealed with dough prepared with all-purpose flour.

Everything is taken to the oven and the cook must be very precise with the cooking times so that both the rice and the seafood are at their exact point. Then the dough is opened and the intoxicating aromas escape to the outside to enamor the diners. There are families that choose to replace seafood with chicken or lamb, it all depends on the economic status.

Although the dish was not typical of Laila's land and her family, Elias learned that it was very popular in Dubai, their new home that had welcomed them. He supposed that, in this process of adaptation, the family's gastronomic options also had to broaden their horizons to blend in with the traditions of their new home.

"The word 'biryani' is of Persian origin and means 'fried before being cooked'," said a familiar voice that suddenly joined the conversation in the living room of that villa in Al Furjan. It was her. It was Laila.

Chapter Eight

Under a Stary Night

"Poetry doesn't want followers, it wants lovers."

Federico Garcia Lorca

The big day had arrived. Elias looked at himself in the mirror and adjusted the knot of his tie. He had chosen a beige silk one, with a delicate pattern. He couldn't help but remember that emerald green tie from his personal collection, which was part of the long list of coincidences he had with that girl he met at an airport. Laila and his story with her, seemed alien, unreal and distant.

Today, on the other hand, he would seal a much more real and close love pact. What would have happened to that airport girl that Elias seemed to be eternally in love with?

When he saw her appear in the living room of her parents' house, Elias felt his breath catch in his throat, his hands become clumsy and shaky, and his heart beat at a speed that threatened to burst out of his chest.

"I've brought you some gifts from Mexico," he said as best he could to break the silence that had settled in the room after her arrival.

"Please, Elias. Sit down. Make yourself comfortable, you're in your own home," Dalida said kindly to show cordiality and ease the slight but noticeable tension that the encounter had triggered. Once seated, Elias began to take out the gifts that had traveled with him from Saltillo. He carefully selected the gifts he would give first.

The first gift was for Dalida. Laila's mother took the square box and from it took out a colorful figure that was wrapped in several layers of delicate tissue paper. "It's an 'alebrije'," Elias told her. A handmade statuette, very typical of Mexican craftsmanship and with a spectacular color.

The small pegasus, made of copal wood and hand-painted with the most minute details, left Dalida pleasantly surprised. She immediately got up to find a special place for it in her living room and from that day on the winged horse found its new home on a shelf, near a photograph of Laila. After showing her appreciation, Dalida would learn that the "alebrijes" had been born from the illness that left a Mexican artist named Pedro Linares López bedridden and that, years later, they had become an essential part of the country's culture.

In 1936, Linares lost consciousness as a result of a strange illness. The family did not have the resources to have him treated by a traditional doctor, so they decided to take care of him at home with homemade healing practices. Pedro Linares fell into a deep sleep state. When he woke up, he would tell that he found himself in a forest full of trees and animals that did not seem to have their normal appearance.

He spoke about a rooster with bull horns, a donkey with wings, and a lion with a dog's head. The animals also spoke and began to shout, in perfect synchrony: "¡Alebrijes!" Pedro ran and ran, until he escaped through a small window. In doing so, he woke up.

Already conscious and back to reality, he wanted to use his skills as a cardboard artist to model these fantastic animals that he had met. He painted them by hand, to emulate their picturesque and bright colors, and without knowing it, he was making an invaluable contribution to the culture and art of his country.

Everyone present seemed fascinated by Elias' story. They found something about his culture, full of fables and colors, completely fascinating.

"If you liked this story, you'll like the one that comes with my next gift even more," he said, smiling and more confident now that he had won over the audience in that room. He reached into his bag and took out a perfectly folded green textile.

He opened it and raised his hands, to display a beautiful green *sarape* with delicate gold thread details, which he had brought from Saltillo. This was a special gift for Hassan.

"I know those," said a male voice. It was Hassan himself, who looked considerably excited by the gift. "Those are like the ones 'Canelo' wears." He was referring to Saul Alvarez, the popular Mexican boxer.

"Well, what do you think? This is called a *sarape* and this one I brought you was made by Hector Tamayo. The same artisan who makes the sarapes that 'Canelo' wears to his fights."

"I can't believe it. Elias, do you like boxing?"

"I love it. It's a big part of my culture and my life".

"Do you think 'Canelo' is the best boxer in history?"

"Well, even though he is Mexican and he is a boxer I admire, I think the title of 'best in history' goes to someone else. For me, it's Muhammad Ali."

"I like you already, Elias. We can get together later to talk more about boxing," Hassan said as he got up to shake the visitor's hand and take the sarape to put it on. "Hey, how do you know about Ali? You weren't even born when he was at his peak as a boxer."

"It's because my dad was a big fan and he would show me fights he had recorded on VHS."

Elias' mind couldn't help but search through dusty memories for a treasured scene. He saw himself as a child in the cozy living room of his parents' house. The darkness of the room was interrupted by the soft glow of the TV screen. The muffled sound of two strong and agile men resonated in the room, while a boxing match unfolded on the screen. That child in the memories had his face barely illuminated by the blue light. His concentration was absolute.

His father, a man passionate about boxing, sat down next to him, his eyes shining with enthusiasm. "Son, do you see that man there? That's Muhammad Ali, the greatest of all time," he said, pointing to the TV with reverence.

Elias' eyes widened with admiration and curiosity: "Muhammad Ali? Is he as good as you say, Dad?"

"Oh, boy! Muhammad Ali is not just a boxer; he is a poet in the ring. Look how he moves, how he dances around his opponents. It's not just brute force, it's intelligence, grace and determination," the father explained with a passionate voice.

The boy watched Ali's every move with attention, captivated by the magic of the moment. "And why is he so great, Dad?"

His father smiled, remembering the legendary boxer's accomplishments. "Because he never gave up, even when life threw its hardest punches at him. Outside the ring, Ali was a man of principle, a defender of justice and equality. He always got back up, no matter how many times he was knocked down. That, my son, is what makes a true champion."

The boy nodded with understanding, his eyes reflecting the spark of inspiration. "I want to be like him, Dad."

His father gave him a loving pat on the shoulder, keeping his eyes on the screen. "Then follow in his footsteps, son. Not just in boxing, but in life. Muhammad Ali taught us that greatness lies in courage, dignity, and perseverance."

The fight continued on the screen, it was a match recorded on VHS and this became a moment that was also recorded and will live forever in the mind of its protagonist.

And from the living room of Elias' parents' house in Saltillo, his mind traveled to the present moment. In the living room of Laila's parents' house. In Dubai.

As he stood there, he remembered that, for Karim and Samia there was also a special gift, considering she had been his most faithful accomplice. For his family he had bought two hammocks, embroidered with colorful threads and fringes. Very typical of the Yucatan region.

He had also brought a gift for Laila. Perhaps the most special of all, but the moment of presenting it would have to wait, because the smell of *biryani*, now served on the dining table, announced that it was time to change rooms.

Everyone got up praising the aroma and sat down in the seats that were already practically assigned, within the family dynamics. Laila and Elias stayed behind everyone and, almost whispering, he said to her: "I also brought something to give you. Several things actually, I'll give them to you later."

The meal went by with pleasant normality. Elias was afraid that the moment would feel uncomfortable, that the silences would take over the table or that he would spill some kind of sauce on the delicate white linen tablecloth. Impeccable. However, his nightmares did not come true. The food was delicious, the company unbeatable and the conversation varied and fluid. Best of all, he didn't leave any traces on the tablecloth.

Dalida, Samia, and Laila got up to clear the table once everyone had finished eating, and within minutes everything was clean and tidy. "Would anyone like coffee or tea?" Dalida asked politely.

"Actually, I had other plans for our honored guest," Samia said. "If you like, I'd like to take you for a walk along the marina. The afternoon is beautiful and I'm sure it will give us a memorable sunset."

Samia's offer was generous. So, after Elias saw Laila nod in agreement, he did the same. He didn't want to take any initiative that would be frowned upon. Laila and Elias got up from the table, thanking Dalida and Hassan for the delicious lunch and for the family time. Laila took her belongings and Samia did the same. Karim took the car keys and invited Elias to ride with him while they waited for the girls.

Upon arriving at the marina, Karim stopped the car and waited for everyone to get out before continuing on his way. He had to pick up the children from school. While he completed this task, which was part of his daily routine, Samia, Laila, and Elias would walk around the area. It was at this moment that Laila revealed to her traveling friend the big secret of how she had obtained his number.

The walk was pleasant, surreal, and fun. It lasted about ninety minutes and ended with a delicious snack in those charming streets lined with canals and docked boats. Karim and the children joined the meeting, who also got to know the Mexican visitor.

They sat down in a nice place called The Coffee Club located inside the marina mall. They chose it because besides loving the coffee they served there, they wanted to show their guest the impressive views that can be seen from the terrace.

The coffees they ordered arrived served in blue cups. They looked creamy and really delicious. Three mochis also appeared on the table, arranged on a layer of crushed pistachios. These were Japanese cakes made with rice dough and filled with ice cream that seemed to have a good reputation in this place.

Laila took the coffee cup with both hands and Elias noticed that they were delicate and small. It amused him that she needed both hands to hold that large cup. He smiled.

When Elias put his cell phone away in his bag, he touched a plastic figurine that he knew was important. It was a toy brontosaurus that he had bought at a flea market in Saltillo and that he had brought for Laila. This was a kind of detail that represented a part of his work, which he enjoyed very much and wanted to share with her. He put it on the table and told her it was for her. Laila looked at it smiling and took the prehistoric figure in her hands.

"Are we going to go extinct? Like the dinosaurs," she said with a laugh.

"I don't know if this will have a happy ending or if we will end up extinct. But today we only have today. And today has been an incredible day."

"What about my sarape?" she asked. Elias replied that he had something better. He had commissioned a delicate white gold plaque, with a tiny diamond at its top and with coordinates engraved: 25° 25' 21.00" N 55° 15' 47.00" E. "And what are these numbers and letters?" she asked with great curiosity.

"These are the exact coordinates of the airport where we met."

Laila smiled and her cheeks blushed for a few minutes. She loved this gift, which besides being beautiful, had a special meaning. This was something she paid attention to, these gifts that were made with effort to offer something more than just "an object". Behind the gold plaque was creativity, thought, and heart. Although she was completely fascinated, she did her best not to burst with emotion and to remain calm, demure, and as she was supposed to be.

"Thank you so much Elias! I love special details."

"I still have another gift for you, but I'll give it to you later. Let it be a surprise."

The golden sun dissolved into the horizon of the picturesque village, casting the remnants of its faint light upon the mosque's dome, the oldest in the entire country. Elias was ready. He met his parents in the small room where he finished getting ready. The three embraced.

"May love be with you forever, son!" his mother said, squeezing his hand in support.

Elias looked up and felt the warmth of the stone-vaulted ceilings. He waited for his parents to leave the small room too and closed the wooden door behind him. They entered a vast hall, its cream-colored stone walls rising to vaulted ceilings. Enormous windows let in the remaining daylight and air to the gathering. The warm glow of the sunset bathed the enormous room in a golden light. The floor was completely covered with Persian carpets, and close relatives were sitting on them. When Elias arrived with his parents, everyone turned to look at them.

The minutes before the Nikah ceremony were filled with a solemn silence in the prayer hall of the mosque, where the remaining guests finished settling down on the adorned carpets. Maria, Elias' mother, entered holding a silver tray with bread and milk. This would be an offering for the bride.

It was impossible for Elias' mind to avoid the journey back to that April day and to that silent room in the house of Laila's parents in Dubai. That day, Elias met with Hassan to ask for his daughter's hand in marriage. Disjointed scenes, like scraps of memory, appeared as flashes in the mind of the future groom. These moments, which for him were accompanied by nervousness, stirred his stomach. He remembered that that day had not ended as he had expected or imagined.

And now he was here, at the point where his destiny had led him, perhaps as a consequence of that conversation charged with tension and nervousness. But for Elias this was not a "perhaps," he was sure that that afternoon, in front of Hassan, a determining page of his story with Laila had been written. For better or for worse.

The imam's booming voice interrupted Elias' reverie, filling the sacred space with melodious verses that spoke of love as a divine gift. The bride and groom approached from opposite ends of the hall, she from the east and he from the west. For the first time that afternoon, their eyes met, sparkling with promises and unspoken vows. Elias felt his chest swell, as if his heart was growing rapidly and trying to escape through his ribs. His future wife looked like an angel, and the scene moved him to tears. Now their hearts beat in unison, echoing the love that had united them.

The chanting ended, and now a hush fell over the atmosphere as the gentle swish of the white dress gracefully announced the bride's official entrance. Her hips were enveloped by a tulle skirt, her torso embraced by a delicate long-sleeved bodice. The elegant lace and beaded embroidery exuded an aura of timeless beauty. Each stitch seemed to tell a chapter of her love story with the man who would soon become her husband.

However, what truly stood out were the details embellishing the bride's hands and feet: intricate henna tattoos. Each stroke was a masterpiece, not only in terms of artistry but also in its cultural and spiritual significance.

These tattoos were not mere decorations; they were symbols meant to ward off evil spirits while also carrying deep and specific meanings. Each curve and line represented a secret language of symbols, understood only by those steeped in tradition.

This fragrant paste, made from the leaves of various herbs, creates an impression on the bride's skin that seems temporary at first glance, but is deeply lasting. These arabesques, drawn on the delicate canvas of the hands, serve as the perfect analogy to define the line that separates the temporal from the eternal, and vain beauty from tradition.

The bride's tattoos are the very imprints of love that will fade from her skin in days, but will remain forever engraved in her heart and soul. Mehndi, as this form of body art is officially called, is a masterpiece in itself, an expression of love that transcends time and beautifies not only the body but also the human essence that will be united with another, for all eternity, through the sacred bond of matrimony.

The white dress, the veil, the flowers, and the henna tattoos were more than just adornments or accessories; they were tangible expressions of the cultural and emotional richness that infused every aspect of the ceremony, transforming it into a visible testimony that spoke of the union that was beginning to be forged, for eternity, between these two lovers.

As the bride walked forward, a group of women gracefully approached to accompany her steps. Their voices began to intertwine in a sweet song that resonated in the air like an ancestral melody. The women's choir, inspired by the beauty and solemnity of the moment, elevated the ceremony to a spiritual level that moved all witnesses.

In that sacred moment, the perfume of the flowers tangled with the emotion that floated in the air. The bride, dressed entirely in white, approached the groom. The veil served to envelop and conceal her face and her grace, especially shielding her face from the gazes of all those present. There, amidst this exuberant and enchanting cultural celebration, stood Elias. Waiting for her, as he had done throughout his life, as fate had ordained, as he had always imagined, to seal the unbreakable pact of love. Everything was ready to begin the ceremony.

The vows were pronounced, each word resonating in the hearts of those who accompanied the bride and groom on this special occasion. He and she promised each other the purest love, the most enriching respect, and the strength of mutual support, committing to walk together on the path of life, sheltered under the most important blessing of all.

The imam shared with them the secret of happiness. He revealed it without holding back, without hesitation, and without selfishness. It turned out that the formula that unlocks this longed-for feeling of fulfillment and ecstasy was simpler than it seems:

"The idea is quite simple, even more than you might have imagined. If both partners in a couple strive daily to make each other happy and satisfied, then they need not directly strive to seek their own happiness."

The reason was that, through this mutual and reciprocal commitment, happiness would naturally come to each one. The key was to know how to invest in the joy of the other, trusting that, in turn, this would eventually become a shared path to personal happiness.

Prayers filled the hall with an enveloping melody. The aromatic vapor of the incense rose in spirals that seemed to want to play with the air for just a few brief seconds. These fumes, steeped in centuries of tradition, not only filled the room with their exquisite fragrances but also carried with them a deep symbolism: purification, warding off evil, and the creation of an atmosphere imbued with sacredness. Tradition has it that aromatic smoke has the power to change or elevate the energy of the space.

The bride, with tears of happiness glistening in her eyes, humbly and gratefully received the blessings that were poured upon her. Each word spoken resonated as an indelible bond between past and future, between centuries-old traditions and a new chapter of love and commitment. Elias, with hands that trembled slightly but were firm in his purpose, reverently slipped the ring onto her finger. In that simple gesture, they sealed their commitment not only in the eyes of the community, but also as a promise offered to God.

Then it was her turn, who could not stop smiling as she handed him the ring. Although the exchange of rings was not a rigorous part of the Nikah ceremony, she knew that for Elias, her great love, this was an important symbolism.

"Do you accept this ring as a symbol of our commitment?"

He extended his hand tenderly, to receive from her the delicate silver ring that had traveled with him from Mexico. "Of course, I accept with all my heart. This ring not only represents our commitment, but also the respect for our traditions and the beauty of our love, which is unique and unrepeatable." Elias' voice trembled.

"It fills me with joy that we are uniting our lives in this way. It means a lot to me that you respect and participate in what defines me and is important to me," she said softly.

"I want to be a part of your whole world, today and always. Of everything you are, which makes me a better person. This ring is more than a symbol; it's a constant reminder of our love that transcends everything humanly possible."

She leaned closer and whispered a message in his ear, as if wanting to keep a detail just for the two of them, despite the appreciation she felt for the company of all present: "This moment is even more special because we share it, not only as a couple, but as two people who love and respect each other."

Elias took her by both hands and whispered back, a symbol of their complicity. "I'm in love with our love, because I consider it unique. And I can't wait to experience what lies ahead with you. To write our story together, on the same page and with the same indelible ink."

The families, witnesses to this sacred union, not only celebrated the love that blossomed between them, but also recognized that, with this symbolic act, the family roots had spread and the branches of the family tree were intertwined in a new and promising network of relationships. The family had grown, and today they celebrated together, without distinction, that the acceptance of the conditions of the marriage contract had taken place.

Attention shifted to the center of the hall, where the bride's respected father stood watching with pride and emotion. Elias humbly approached him, formally requesting his beloved's hand in marriage. The gesture resonated with traditions of respect and commitment, and that man with a thick white beard and olive-green eyes, which filled with tears, gave his blessing to his daughter's union.

The mosque vibrated with applause and joy as the newly married couple emerged, enveloped in a warm light that bathed them as they emerged. The doors of the religious building opened and those present stepped out to revel in the night sky, which was studded with stars.

In that magical setting, the love story, which now had a happy ending (or a beginning), was revealed as a masterpiece that would remain woven deeply and intrinsically into those mosque carpets. Each knot, each detail, spoke of the time and patience invested in merging two seemingly different worlds into perfect harmony.

That night, under the benevolent gaze of the stars, was marked as a transcendental chapter in their story. A story that was the purest testament to the power of love. Love that could create bridges where before there were only barriers, and unite hearts in an eternal dance that would resonate throughout the generations.

On that starry night, the world seemed to shrink. It was only him and her. But who was this girl under the veil? Was it Laila? What had transpired during the proposal to Hassan? These questions swirled in the air, and the truth would soon be revealed.

The setting sun cast its golden light on the backyard of Hassan's house, creating dancing shadows on the terracotta walls. These were the same walls he'd helped build, the silent witnesses to his daughters' childhood. Elias approached him. Although he had proven himself to be a good man and the reception had been warm and kind so far, he knew that the moment of truth had arrived. Decisive minutes and words that would spin the roulette of their lives. He could feel his legs trembling, as if he had to force himself with every step closer to him. That imposing gentleman with a thick white beard. He was afraid of tripping.

Elias wore a clean, light-colored suit that was perfectly ironed. His shirt was a subtle lilac shade, and in one of the inner pockets of his jacket, he kept a jade stone for good luck. The smooth green mineral had been a gift from her. From Laila.

She had given it to him the night before when they said goodbye. Each in their corresponding standing spot. No hugs. No kisses. Not even a pat on the back. She could anticipate the tension that was beginning to build in the atmosphere after spending idyllic days visiting and sightseeing in Dubai. Laila knew that the coming day would be decisive. "Are you talking to Dad tomorrow. Right?" she asked with a hint of anguish in her voice.

Elias nodded his head repeatedly. A knot of anxiety tightened in his throat, rendering him speechless. In his most private thoughts, those he never shared with her, he felt like taking her hand, running out into the street, taking a taxi and escaping far away. To a place so remote that Hassan could no longer influence their decisions. But he knew that this illusion was childish and cowardly.

"A jade. For good luck," she said. Elias stretched out his hand and turned his wrist so that his palm faced the sky. She placed the cold stone in his hand, and he closed his fingers around it, rubbing it with his thumb. "It's a lucky jade. But no matter how much you rub it, you won't make a genie appear to grant you the wish of not having to face my father tomorrow," Laila said with a laugh. It was as if she could read his mind and travel to those dark and dusty corners where he kept his most private thoughts. His most primal instincts and his most childish reactions.

"Thank you, Laila! I'm going to need it," he replied, smiling at her. "Hey! Before I forget... Remember I told you I had another gift for you?"

"I remember. Yes."

"Well, here it goes." Elias took off his backpack, unzipped it, and reached into the bag. He pulled out two books from the bottom. "Let's see, this first one is a special edition of *Gone With the Wind* (by Margaret Mitchell). It used to be mine, but now I want it to be yours."

"Elias! You can't be serious! I remember telling you in one of our many conversations that it was a book I was waiting to read."

"Now this book is something that will always remind me of you. But..."

Laila interrupted him. "But what? Elias, what else are you going to give me? You're making me nervous with your mystery."

"I'll always try to give you everything. But while I can't do that..." Elias picked up the second book, which was resting under the thick, heavy edition of the novel. It was a book with a purple and emerald green cover, featuring a woman wearing a hijab and standing with her back to the reader. The title spelled out her name: "Laila."

She took it in her hands, confused, and when she turned to the first page, she found a handwritten dedication:

"To Laila. The real-life one.

The one who transcends fiction and geographical, physical and heart barriers."

"You've left me speechless. You wrote me a book?"

"It's only logical that you have the first edition of the book you inspired, the one I named after you. Maybe by tomorrow you'll end the day as my girlfriend," Elias said as he took his leave.

Now feeling the jade with his fingers inside his jacket pocket, he gathered his strength and finished walking towards the house's patio. Hassan was sitting in a wicker chair, quietly watching the sunset colors work their magic on his garden. Upon seeing Elias, he offered a warm smile and gestured for him to sit next to him.

"Elias, my son, how are you?" Hassan asked, extending his hand to greet him.

Elias took Hassan's hand respectfully and nodded as he looked for a seat close to him. "I'm fine, thank you. But there's something important I want to discuss with you sir."

Hassan asked him to continue but to please not refer to him as simply Hassan, and forget the formalities of the "sir". He explained that it made him feel older.

"I'm here to talk about Laila," Elias began. His words had been carefully chosen before the meeting. "From the moment I met her, I knew she was someone special. She's an incredibly strong, intelligent, and beautiful woman. Every day by her side, whether near or far, is a divine gift, and I've realized that I can't imagine my life without her."

Elias expected an immediate response, but instead he was met with silence. A heavy silence descended upon the terrace, like a heavy blanket descending on those present after Elias revealed his intention to marry Laila to Hassan. The air became dense with unspoken tension, and both their faces reflected a mixture of surprise and bewilderment. The revelation had created a palpable void, a space where words hung suspended in the air, afraid to break the fragile stillness that had settled between the two men.

Their gazes began to shift and avoid each other, as if both were trying to find refuge in any corner of that green garden that was not burdened with the newly exposed reality. Elias, aware of the discomfort floating around him, searched in vain for the right words to dissolve it.

Fidgeting and avoiding eye contact, Elias prolonged the discomfort. The atmosphere was heavy, each second stretching into an eternity as time seemed to stand still, accommodating the unease that reigned in the room.

He could do nothing but reach for the jade resting in his jacket pocket. He grasped it and rubbed it with his fingers, recalling Laila's joke about the genie. Perhaps, at this moment, that was exactly what he needed. A genie to grant him a wish, or even a miracle.

The occasional nervous cough or the creak of a chair barely broke the silence, doing little to alleviate the tension. The two men clung to the hope that someone, at some point, would raise their voice and free the room from its suffocating grip. However, the silence persisted, transforming the atmosphere into a minefield of unmet expectations and newfound realities.

Elias decided to cut through the tension with the sharp sword of his words. "I ask for your permission and blessing to marry Laila. You see, I love her with all my heart and I promise to cherish her, respect her, and be her support in all circumstances. I want to build a home with her filled with love and understanding. I want a family like the one you built. And I believe that together we could face any challenge that life throws our way. Because I feel that life wants us together."

Hassan remained silent for a moment, as if carefully considering every word that came out of Elias' mouth.

Chapter Nine

An Unforgettable Party

"What do you want? You want the moon? Just say the word
and I'll throw a lasso around it and pull it down."

George Bailey, *It's A Wonderful Life*

On the shores of the Mediterranean, where the sun and moon take turns gazing at their reflections on the tranquil waters and mountains guard the land with centuries of stories, stood a majestic mansion that would be the chosen place to celebrate love. The sun had set, giving the couple a beautiful sunset during the ceremony that took place in an ancient mosque. The wind blew through the thousand-year-old cedars, announcing the union of two souls that would be together until the end of their existence on earth.

The main entrance of the monumental house was covered in flowers and foliage, a [breathtaking/ethereal/luscious] creation by a local company called Exotica. Each petal, each flower, and each branch were placed with decorative intent, and each color and aroma helped transform the everyday scene into a garden of dreams.

Delicate pastel flowers were hung upside down, from their stems, starting from the ceilings. This visual spectacle welcomed the guests and guided them towards the heart of the floral eden. Intoxicating fragrances floated in the air, as if the flowers themselves were capable of whispering blessings and greetings to the arriving guests.

Elias, impeccably dressed and groomed, waited at the threshold with his entourage of friends. Some were relatives of his now-wife and others were his "compas", his lifelong friends who had flown from Mexico to accompany him on the adventure of "I do". They all seemed to follow a strict dress code: hair slicked back so that no hair dared to step out of bounds, tailor-made suits, silk ties, and shiny patent leather shoes.

In the distance, the drums of the *Zaffa* resonated like the heartbeat of the celebration, announcing with each beat that a defining moment of every wedding was approaching: the entrance of the bride and groom.

The soft beats of the music joined the beating of the leather of each drum. The result was a joyful symphony that lifted the spirits of the attendees. The bride, wrapped in the grace of a delicate dress that seemed to be woven from the threads of the constellations, appeared at the main entrance. Her veil, as light as moonlight, fluttered with each step, while the flower petals danced around her like faithful companions on her journey.

The guests, dressed in colors reminiscent of the warm hues of the sunset, watched in wonder. The women wore dresses that seemed to reflect the richness of floral fields, and the men, proud in their traditional attire, exuded an elegance that only the blend of cultures could achieve.

The *Zaffa*, with its drums and cymbals, marked the entrance of the bride and groom into the heart of the celebration. The *Dabke* dancers, in a display of energy and skill, joined the procession, bringing with them the vitality of the celebration. It was not the first time that Elias had experienced this exciting moment, so classic of Arab weddings. His father had taken care to let him know the resounding emotion that the drumming produces and how this tradition had the power to take him back to the early years of his life. To his childhood in Lebanon, during those years when his father, Elias' grandfather, had not made the decision to move to North America in search of better opportunities.

Elias had also seen a *Dabke* live at the various weddings of the Arab community he attended in Saltillo. But this time he was the protagonist of this moment and the emotion escalated through his chest with each beat of the drum. His friends, lost in the face of the powerful dance, did not yet know how to react. But, little by little, they let themselves be carried away by the captivating rhythms of the Middle East and ended up being part of that united line of men who held each other's shoulders and hands.

This was not just any euphoric party dance; this line was a way to create a symbolic connection between the participants. All you had to do was join in and let yourself be carried away by the intense percussive rhythms of the *derbakke* (drum) and start making energetic steps, lifting and hitting your feet against the ground to the rhythm of the music.

The most experienced dancers began to show off with jumping movements, turns and lateral movements. But they did everything trying to preserve the harmony of the music and the pulsating vibe of the group.

Elias, in the midst of powerful footsteps, turned to look at his bride and was completely entranced by her beauty. The two seemed to be living in their own world where emotions were shared. They walked among the guests, who waited for them with their faces illuminated by smiles of admiration.

Then he began to remember the ceremony of just a few hours ago, led by the imam who, with his wise prayers, had made that day unforgettable. A sacred ritual where promises of love were intertwined with the ancient history of the land that welcomed them.

The dances and festivities opened the appetites of those present, so the great banquet was announced, which unfolded in a feast of Mediterranean flavors and aromas.

The food at the party was an important point for the parents, who were in charge of organizing the feast. And for them, food was much more than exquisite snacks to please the palate of their loved ones and guests. The banquet was a sign of generosity and hospitality. That is why the host families made an effort to serve a table with an extensive variety of dishes that would delight the senses and bring all the diners together around the feast.

The long banquet table was decorated with exquisite lace and luxurious fabrics. Candles flickered on trays, creating an intimate atmosphere where guests shared laughter and toasts to a love that would grow strong, like the cedars that guarded the land.

At the center of the table, platters of couscous, *pilaf* rice, rice with almonds and pine nuts, and seasoned lamb meatballs tempted diners. There was also a variety of fish and seafood, prepared with aromatic spices. The *mezze* station offered a rich selection of spreads like *hummu*s and *baba ganoush*, grape leaves stuffed with rice and nuts, and an array of dips, olive oil, and herbs. The tantalizing aroma of freshly baked bread wafted through the air, drawing new diners to the enormous baskets brimming with warm pita bread.

In honor of the bride and her mother, who had a sweet tooth, the dessert table stood out with silver trays overflowing with *baklava*, *ma'amoul*, and *knafeh*, dates, and fresh fruits. Elias managed to sneak some churros onto the table, to be enjoyed with chocolate and "cajeta". It was his favorite dessert and he couldn't wait for his wife to try them. When she tasted their crispy texture and the perfect balance of sweet and savory, she would start to share this sweet indulgence with him.

The food seemed to have energized everyone to continue dancing all night long. The *Dabke* carried the energy of the celebration, and other dances joined in. The energetic couple, amidst colored lights and dancing shadows, found in music the perfect expression to manifest the emotion they felt in their hearts. Faced with something that was practically impossible to describe in words, it was better to dance to let out the emotion.

In this corner of the world, under a blanket of twinkling stars, the wedding became an unforgettable chapter in their lives. A fusion of traditions, the magic of flavors, the resounding drums, and the energy of those dances formed the backdrop for a love that promised an exciting future, left its mark on the souls of those who witnessed this majestic union. The imposing mansion, as a silent witness, would forever keep, within its walls, the echoes of the celebration, perpetuating the magic of that night in the collective memory of those who had witnessed a love that transcended all barriers.

Amidst the incomparable euphoria, Elias took his wife by the hand and led her down one of the corridors to a terrace. He wanted a moment of intimacy to talk to her.

"Who would have thought that after one date, we would end up being husband and wife?" he said, holding her hands in his. He noticed how cold they were and asked if she was feeling chilly.

"No, I'm fine," she said with a laugh. "Maybe it's just nerves. You still make me nervous, Elias. Can you believe that?"

"Yes, I can believe it. The same thing happens to me every time I see you. But I imagine that, little by little, we'll get used to being together."

"We're already husband and wife!" she said excitedly.

"We're already husband and wife!" he said, dazzled.

The newlyweds kissed. It was their second kiss of the night and also their second officially as husband and wife. Hand in hand, they returned to the party and disappeared into the crowd of guests flooding the dance floor.

Chapter Ten

The Knot

"Whatever our souls are made of, his and mine are the
same."

Emily Brontë

Hassan was silent for a moment, as if weighing Elias' words and his proposal, or rather his intentions to marry his daughter. Fortunately, after smiling frankly, he said:

"Elias, I have always believed that love and respect are the foundation of a strong marriage. I hear your words and, in your voice, I can perceive that honest tone that reassures me. In your eyes, I can see the deep love you have for my daughter. I can also see myself reflected in them. I see myself at your age, with the dreamy enthusiasm of youth, when I had to approach my father-in-law to marry Dalida. It seems incredible today, but I was also nervous, sweaty, and in your position."

"And I thought I was hiding my nerves well," Elias said, letting out a liberating laugh that they both shared. The laughter eased the tension in the air.

"And, honestly, the love for Laila is something I appreciate more than anything else. I accept your request with joy and give my blessing for you to become a part of our family."

Elias sighed with relief and gratitude. "Thank you, Hassan. I promise I will do everything I can to be the husband Laila deserves and that you trust me to be."

Hassan stood up and shook Elias' hand. "Welcome to the family, son. May your marriage be filled with love, understanding, and happiness. From my side, I promise you will be like the son I never had."

"Thank you, Sir… Sorry, Hassan. With all due respect, I admire you for the person you are and for raising a woman like Laila. Especially after she told me she admired Muhammad Ali and his words took me straight back to my childhood and those fights I enjoyed watching with my dad."

"Elias, do you know the name of the boxer's daughter? The one who is precisely the most well-known and admired of the nine he had?"

"Laila?" Elias said with doubt in his voice.

"That's right. Her name is Laila. And that's why I chose that name for my second daughter. I like to think that she is not a dark night, but rather like a beautiful starry night."

Hassan's comment came from the fact that the name he chose for his daughter came from the derivative of *Layl,* which in Arabic means "night."

"And I promise to take care of her like a star. The brightest in my sky."

After hearing the young Elias' words, Hassan couldn't help but invite him to cement their bond with a strong hug.

The sunset light seemed to shine with a special glow as Elias walked away from the garden, carrying with him the promise of a shared future with the woman he loved.

Leaving, knowing she had said yes, was the most beautiful and gratifying of all surprises, and the most favorable scenario. He knew that fate had to have had a hand in this.

Elias could not have imagined that after that April and that risky trip to Dubai to overcome a seemingly impossible goal, he would only have to wait seven months to hug and kiss Laila for the first time. They would do it on November 24th, which was the date they had chosen together for their wedding.

That day was significant because it was the day they met, for just a few seconds, in New York. A failed attempt at a meeting, a slap in the face from fate. A precious lesson learned the hard way: that occasion was the greatest representation of how little control we have over the strings of life.

It was a day when both would begin to understand that, on the great stage of existence, the human being perceives himself as the skillful puppeteer of his own marionette, believing that his decisions and actions are like the strings he can pull to take control of the show. However, in the darkness of that illusion and behind the thick red curtain, a deeper truth is revealed: Destiny, like a great invisible director, is really the one who is in charge of handling the strings that lead us through the journey we have decided to call life.

Each choice, each step taken with determination, may seem like a manifestation of control, but in reality, they are the responses to a script that unfolds before us. The game of decisions takes us down unforeseen paths, revealing that we are rather the ones who occupy the passenger seat on the journey.

Learning to be passengers implies letting go of the reins of absolute control. Getting into the taxi, closing the door, letting the road decide. It is embracing uncertainty with courage, because it is recognized that, although we may not have ultimate control, we can still influence the narrative of our own story. Each unexpected turn, each surprise that fate offers us, is an invitation to be aware of our role as active participants in the flow of our existence on planet Earth.

Instead of resisting the power of fate, one can better learn to enjoy the journey, delighting in the complexity of each turn and each new path. Being co-pilots means admiring the beauty of the landscape, even when the route becomes unexpected. In this understanding, we find the freedom to let go of the tension of controlling everything and, instead, blindly embrace the wonder of the unknown.

In the vast theater of existence, we become accomplices to our destiny, enriching our lives with the wisdom that, while we cannot direct the show, we can choose how to dance within it. With each conscious choice, each shared laugh, and each tear shed, we become architects of our own meaning, co-authors of a story that unfolds with grace, and grateful apprentices of the eternal dance of destiny.

After their whirlwind romance that began in New York and blossomed during a challenging trip to Dubai, Elias and Laila had to face a temporary separation. If Elias and Laila had not surrendered to this dance beyond their control, they would not have come so far. But in doing so, they were able to savor the sweetness of what would come after. All for being patient, for believing, and for waiting.

Elias said goodbye to Laila at the entrance of the Dubai airport. A place that was not as spectacular as Chabrouh Dam, but had something that not even the most beautiful landscape on the planet had: it was "theirs." It felt like their own, or like a secret they shared in the mystery of silence.

"See you in November. The next time I see you, it will be for life."

Laila blushed, but said goodbye with the thought of surviving those seven months apart thanks to the promise of that kiss that would seal the pact of love between them.

"I can't wait for that moment either. I dream of being able to hug you, Elias."

That first hug between Laila and Elias marked the culmination of a wait filled with respect and dedication. After a wedding ceremony steeped in tradition and family ties, they finally found themselves in an intimate corner. Laila, radiant in her wedding dress, and Elias, with a mixture of emotion and respect in his eyes, dedicated themselves to sharing a connection that transcended words.

The moment unfolded with a delicacy that could only arise from a deep mutual understanding and respect for each other's beliefs. As their bodies drew closer, an electric current ran down their spines and traveled to every corner of their nervous bodies. Elias, with care and reverence, wrapped his arms around Laila, feeling her warm response as the first embrace closed like the knot of a red thread that had waited a long time to be tied.

In that embrace, the barriers erected by culture and tradition melted away, leaving space for pure human connection. Laila felt the security of Elias' arms, and he experienced the warmth of mutual acceptance. In that instant, the red thread of destiny, which had woven its way through their lives, enveloped them and knotted itself into an unbreakable bond that united their destinies in a unique and meaningful way. He could smell her, and her scent was as sweet as he had anticipated in his thoughts. She did the same and felt at home.

Every second of the embrace resonated with the magic of anticipation fulfilled. It was more than a physical gesture; it was the materialization of a love that had blossomed despite differences and barriers, a love that, like the red thread, had found its point of convergence in that meaningful physical encounter.

The embrace was followed by the seal of the love pact through their lips. The first kiss was a chapter in their love story written with the ink of anticipation and sweet tension. It happened, as everything with them did, as if the universe itself conspired to unite their lips in an encounter that would resonate forever in their memories.

Elias noticed that his wife's lips, soft and delicate, were unfamiliar, yet at the same time seemed to have the particular taste of the everyday. That feeling of familiarity, as if they had been meant to be together all along. He had never tasted them before, but now everything fit together and it seemed like their connection had always been there, waiting to be discovered.

It was in an intimate corner, far from prying eyes but surrounded by the complicit energy of the surroundings. Their hearts beat in a symphony of emotions, as if they were tuning in to the unique frequency of their connection. Elias, with his tender gaze, sought approval in Laila's eyes, who responded with a smile that spoke volumes.

The first touch of their lips was soft, like the caress of a breeze on the skin. It was a kiss full of meaning, a silent language that spoke of the bond they had cultivated and the unspoken promises whispered in their hearts.

Every inch of that kiss was a journey in itself, exploring uncharted territories and unraveling the layers of contained passion. The whispers of the breeze and the pounding of their hearts created a unique melody, a soundtrack that accompanied them in that moment.

After that kiss, the world seemed to have acquired new shades, as if the act of joining their lips had unlocked a door to a realm of infinite possibilities.

It was the starting point of a love story that would continue to be written with every caress and every shared gaze. In that kiss, Elias and Laila discovered the depth of their connection, inaugurating a chapter of intimacy that, although fleeting in its duration, would resonate eternally in the plot of their shared story.

"Yes. I would like us to spend some time with my grandparents before they leave. I'm so happy that I was able to share my wedding moment with my grandmother Jamila present. It's priceless that she got to see me in my wedding dress and… Completely happy," Laila said tenderly. "That's something I'll always be grateful for, and it shows the great love I know you have for me. The fact that you crossed seas and stepped out of your comfort zone, giving up celebrating your wedding in your own country, with your own people, just for me. I love you, Elias."

"I do it because I love you, Laila."

Chapter Eleven

Honey Moon

"Nobody has ever measured, even poets,

how much a heart can hold."

Zelda Fitzgerald

She gazed out of the car window, taking in the deep blue waters of Jounieh Bay. This was a destination she had long wanted to visit, and now she would be exploring it with her husband. Excitement sat beside her in the passenger seat. But so did fear. This was the first time she would be alone with him. With Elias. With her husband. It felt strange to even think about that word, now that it defined him in relation to her.

"It's beautiful! We're definitely going to have an unforgettable honeymoon," Elias said, taking her hand. His grip turned into a strong, clumsy squeeze. He too had packed a bundle of nerves for their vacation, and now that they could touch each other, freedom felt strange. It was like the elephant in the room or the monster under the bed.

As if both of them, in silence, were waiting for something or someone to suddenly and unexpectedly arrive, to change the rules of the game and return them to the first phase of their relationship, when they had to restrain themselves to achieve what they now had: a sacred love.

November was the perfect season to visit Jounieh, located about 18 kilometers north of Beirut. Sheltered by mountains and with a wide opening to the Mediterranean Sea, the destination was a dream for tourists seeking a beach and nightlife atmosphere during the summer months. In June, July, and August, the place was packed with tourists, but now this privileged and nature-pampered spot belonged, practically, to Elias and Laila.

She had always wanted to see the beaches of Jounieh, but after changing her residence and leaving Lebanon at a young age, the trip had been put on hold on her list. So, Elias, who always paid attention to everything she said, took note and surprised her with this destination. He also wanted her to feel comfortable and "at home," because they had both decided to move to Mexico once they were married. A few months ago, while Elias was finishing up his arrangements to leave Saltillo for a few months and marry Laila, with the promise of bringing her to live in his city after the honeymoon, he made reservations at one of the best hotels in the area: the Bel Azur.

While the Bel Azur was not the most modern or luxurious, it was a classic in Jounieh and had a prime location, very close to the *plage* (beach). Elias learned through research and reservations that just two kilometers from the city was the Casino du Liban, which had been very popular with tourists in the 1960s. He didn't plan to visit, but the image of Laila channeling her inner Ingrid Bergman, and himself as a Humphrey Bogart at the *Casablanca*-esque casino, sparked a playful fantasy.

He envisioned Laila in a long, burgundy velvet dress, with the sophistication and charm of Hollywood's golden era. The fabric, barely fitted, delicately highlighted her figure, while the dark color enhanced the warmth of her skin and the sparkle of her eyes. On the other hand, he could visualize himself with that deep gaze, à la Bogart. He imagined himself wearing an elegant black tuxedo, with a bow tie and a fedora hat, which gave him an air of mystery and classic appeal. His beard, his most characteristic feature, accentuated his square jaw, and suggested the wisdom and charm of a modern gentleman.

As they walked through the luxurious corridors of that place that truly belonged to Elias' imagination, the couple radiated the elegance and glamour that evoked the Casablanca era. Laila, with her refined bearing, seemed to have stepped straight out of a black and white movie, while Elias personified the intrepid and seductive spirit of the heroes of classic cinema. Together, they were a timeless image of romance and style amidst the majesty of the casino, as if they had been transported to an iconic scene from the big screen.

After fantasizing, Elias returned to reality and, nimbly moving his fingers on the keyboard of his computer, finalized the travel details.

Settling into their hotel room, Elias and Laila found a cozy spot on the terrace. With privileged views of the pool and the beach, they stretched out on the chairs to await the sunset's arrival. The sun slowly sank below the horizon, painting the sky pink.

"Would you like to go for a walk on the beach, while we make the most of the last rays of natural light? It's beautiful," she proposed, and he agreed. So, Laila and Elias walked a few meters until they reached the beach, and seeing how short the distance was, Elias was happy with the decision to have chosen this hotel for their stay.

Holding hands (an activity that felt as new as it was exciting), they began their leisurely walk along the Jounieh beach, feeling the soft sand under their bare feet. It was still warm. The weather was perfect: not too hot, not too cold, and not too humid. The hot summer days were already over and the drop in temperature was perfect.

"It still feels surreal to me that we're here, holding hands and walking together in this romantic place. Finally, our honeymoon," Laila said excitedly.

Elias gazed at her with overflowing love. "It's incredible. I never imagined this day would come." They both stopped and turned their bodies to face the sea. The soft sound of the waves lulled them for a few seconds.

"All this beauty leaves me speechless. And to think we're sharing this moment together," Laila said to her husband.

"I'll never forget the day we met. Now, here we are, husband and wife," he said as they gazed deeply into each other's eyes.

"I feel like I'm dreaming. I can't believe we're finally married," she said with a nervous laugh.

"It's real, Laila. And every day I want to remind you how grateful I am to have you by my side," he said, tenderly stroking her back. The sea breeze caressed her too, transporting her back to childhood days spent on Raouche's boardwalk, a place that always felt like a safe haven. Here, with Elias, she felt that same sense of security.

The sun sank into the sea, as if the tons of deep water had managed to melt the star's fire, extinguishing it for a few hours. The newlyweds then walked to their room, which would be their home during their stay. A soft candlelight illuminated the space, creating a cozy atmosphere. Laila blushed. All she could manage to say was, "This place is wonderful!"

Elias approached her slowly, like someone approaching a little bird to appreciate it up close, and walked with the subtlety of someone exploring a minefield. He didn't want to make any false move that would scare her away. He didn't want the little bird to suddenly fly away and escape. He feared, more than anything in the world, losing her.

He took her hands, noticing that they were again icy cold. The sensation was like touching a bronze statue in the cold hall of a museum. He whispered in her ear: "I want these days to be the most special in the world, Laila. That even when we die, even if we live other lives, even if we have other skin, even if we survive the zombie invasion, we will never forget them," he finished the sentence with a laugh. "I want this trip to stay with us like a tattoo."

"So... Are you going to make a bad joke about tattoos too?" she asked, letting out a spontaneous laugh.

"No! I promise to stay very quiet now."

Laila felt her heart race like a *derbakke* (a small, goblet-shaped drum) and then she felt Elias' soft lips stealing a shy kiss. It was one of their first kisses, but also one of many they would share. "That was...", Laila whispered, "That was perfect."

The newlyweds stood there, embraced by the window, watching the moon reflect on the sea, shimmering like a scattered handful of silver coins. Laila and Elias' love reached its fullness on that magical November night on the tranquil shores of the Mediterranean Sea in Jounieh. The gentle whisper of the waves seemed to accompany the melody of their hearts merging into a single beat.

The next morning, after a delicious breakfast at the hotel buffet, Elias began to reveal that he had an itinerary with surprise activities for each day. A driver would be arriving in ten minutes to whisk them away to their first surprise destination.

"Will I have five minutes to get my things from the room?" she asked in a playful tone as if she were a cadet following the orders of her strict and punctual lieutenant colonel.

"Don't take too long, Mrs. Mansour," Elias said, playing along.

Laila jumped slightly at the sound of her new name. "Mrs. Mansour," she repeated in her head, and immediately felt her heart flutter for a few seconds.

"I'll wait for you in the lobby."

"See you there in five minutes."

After a short car ride, they arrived at the base of the famous *Téléphérique*. They boarded a tiny, vibrant red cabin and began the ascent. It was breathtaking to see how this small, cable-guided compartment traversed the city's buildings, weaving through narrow spaces and then rising to leave the concrete behind and open up to a spectacular view of the blue sea.

"How beautiful," she said, looking out at the sea that now stood between the city buildings.

"Not bad," he replied, as if the visual spectacle was not enough for him.

"Did you expect more, my lieutenant colonel?" she said with a mischievous laugh, as if wanting this to become a coded joke that would be "very them."

"Don't misunderstand me. It's just that I wouldn't dare use the word 'beautiful'," he continued. "Especially when you're here by my side and the point of comparison is enormous."

She smiled and took advantage of the moment of solitude, the view, the place, and the activity to intertwine her fingers with his. She said nothing, in fact, she used the silence to make sure that this moment, which felt unique and special, was stored, almost photographically, in some little part of her memory.

The journey lasted just under ten minutes. Upon reaching the top, they felt the air refresh and bought a souvenir photo of their experience inside the cable car cabin. Elias thought about the perfect place to put it in their Saltillo apartment once they arrived.

Hand in hand, they set off on a walk through a path, filled with stone steps that harmoniously blended with the natural greenery of the mountain. Each spot served as a magical lookout point to savor and absorb the beauty that Joünié gifts to its visitors. After traversing what seemed like a labyrinth of stairs, terraces, and kiosks emitting delightful scents of various simple culinary offerings, Laila and Elias arrived at the point where the ascent continued. This time, it wasn't through a cable car, but a funicular. She had never been on one, despite watching countless videos on social media and was excited. Meanwhile, Elias was thankful for not being suspended from a cable but rather being in contact with rails on the ground.

At the end of the ride, they reached the highest point of the mountain and the views made the journey worthwhile. The sea looked so calm and so blue, it looked like turquoise. The city, with its concrete buildings galore, seemed to rest on a blue plate, in a harmonious coexistence. And then, the colorful paragliders appeared, to make that panorama a true spectacle.

"Would you like to fly a paraglider?" Elias asked his wife.

"You know," she replied with a pause, "I'd love to. It's one of those activities that, even though it scares me a little, I don't want to pass up if I have the chance."

"Would you like us to do it together, for the first time, during our honeymoon?" he asked.

"I'd love to."

"Then we have a date."

The next morning, Laila woke up to the warmth of the first rays of the sun that ushered in the dawn. Turning, she noticed that she was alone in that huge hotel bed, which felt as soft and fluffy as a cloud. "Elias?" she asked, noticing his absence. Then her fingers found a piece of paper between the sheets.

Dear wife,

To start the morning off right, I went to buy you breakfast. The hotel buffet is good,
but we deserve something delicious for today.

Your husband,

Elias

Now Laila was dying of curiosity and excitement, and just when she was about to open the door to the anxiety of having to wait to find out what this surprise was all about, she felt that the door that was opening was the one to the room. Elias had arrived, but... he was empty-handed.

"Good morning, love! What a lovely surprise, but where's the food?" she laughed.

"Someone woke up hungry, didn't you?" he chuckled in response. "Well, get dressed, Mrs. Mansour. I'll be waiting downstairs for breakfast by the seaside."

Laila hastily dressed; her stomach was the one giving orders to her body. She left the room and descended the stairs. Waiting for the elevator was too much. She crossed the lobby, resembling a medieval castle with its light stone walls and tapestries hanging from them. She stepped out the door, found the pool, and in the distance, on the sand, she saw Elias sitting at a table. A hotel waiter was helping him with final adjustments.

She appreciated starting her morning feeling the sand between her now bare toes. The sand felt slightly cold, which was logical after being bathed all night by the moon, who watched over it during those hours.

As she approached, she noticed a feast on the table: lentil Kebbi, scrambled eggs with lamb, mini hotcakes, sweet crepes with strawberries, banana, and chocolate hazelnut cream, pita bread, and spreads. Everything looked delicious, and most importantly, everything was beautifully served.

"Wow, Elias! You're full of surprises. Thank you!"

"Your happiness is my happiness, so... always at your service!"

"It looks delicious!"

"And you have no idea how beautiful the place where I bought it is. Now we have to go to dinner one of these nights."

"If it looks as good as this food tastes, it must be a beautiful place."

"Well, eat up, because now we need to have strength for the next surprise, I have planned for us," Elias requested affectionately.

The same driver who had taken them to the *Téléphérique* the day before appeared at the hotel entrance again. He greeted them kindly as they both got into his car.

"Today's journey will be a bit longer, about twenty minutes, but it will be worth it," commented Rabih, the driver, in a friendly and approachable tone.

As they got out of the car, Laila knew they would be exploring the Jeita Grotto, a two-level karst cave with underground rivers, impressive rock formations, and a significant number of stalactites and stalagmites. "Elias, you won't believe it. But I came to this place when I was just a child, and I've dreamed of coming back as an adult, to appreciate this place that seemed so mystical to me with different eyes," Laila said with an excitement evident in her voice.

The day began by traversing the first cave through walkways, and after finishing the tour, the best part began: a short journey on a wooden train to the second cave, where the *Nahr el-Kalb* River passes through, which means "river of the dog" in Arabic. This stream of water that originates in the mountains of Lebanon and flows into the Mediterranean Sea is navigable in its underground stretch, so the newlyweds were able to enjoy a boat trip through this second cave.

"This is impressive, I feel like I'm in a scene from *The Lord of the Rings*."

"It's true!" Laila replied, laughing. "It's as magical as I remembered."

That night, Laila and Elias dressed up to go out to dinner. On one of the cliffs of Jounieh, a luxurious structure with a French appearance stood imposingly. It was a very famous place in the area that combined the best of French gastronomy with traditional Arab cuisine. Elias had made a reservation, so they were promptly escorted to their table. The place was huge, white, elegant, beautiful. However, he had chosen a simple table on the terrace because the views were spectacular, and the sea breeze would give a unique touch to the dinner.

"What do you think if we go paragliding tomorrow?" Laila asked suddenly.

"Really?

"Yes. I mean, I'm asking you because we talked about it when we saw them flying from the Jounieh viewpoint a few days ago."

"Oh, Laila. The truth is, you're also a box of surprises, '*habibti*'."

"I love how that word sounds when you say it to me," she replied.

On the Wings of Love

The beach of Jounieh stretched out before them, bathed in the golden light of the rising sun. The paragliders, like majestic mechanical birds, waited impatiently to be unfolded. Laila and Elias faced their next challenge, adorned with harnesses and surrounded by the palpable excitement in the air and within their chests. The instructor, an experienced man with eyes reflecting passion for flight, shared some key instructions with enthusiasm. Laila made every effort to listen to his words. It was challenging for her, especially when the beating of her heart reverberated in her head like a powerful instrument, barely allowing her to hear the sounds of her surroundings. Elias, noticing her nerves, sought to reassure her with a complicit look while soothing the butterflies that began to flutter in his stomach.

They weren't the only ones to start flying, as with the parachutes deployed and the harnesses tightened, the couple prepared for takeoff. The wind whispered secrets of freedom, and the warmth of the sun caressed their faces as they walked towards the edge of the beach. Elias took Laila's hand securely, sharing a gesture of complicity before embarking on a new adventure together.

The moment they lifted off the ground, marked the beginning of a unique experience. The sensation of weightlessness filled up their bodies, and the view from the heights unfolded like a magical canvas. The waves of the sea seemed to dance to the rhythm imposed by the music made by the wind, and the mountains loomed in the distance like the silent guardians of that dreamy city.

"It's like we're touching the sky!" exclaimed Laila, letting her eyes moisten with tears that came from within her.

As they floated in the sky of Jounieh, the couple immersed themselves in a silence full of complicity. Sometimes, the impression feels like silence. The absence of words, because they are unnecessary. The sound of the wind and the gentle brushing of the waves created a celestial symphony around them. Elias closed his eyes for a moment, to absorb the feeling of freedom that only an activity like flying can give to a mortal human being.

Then he, always attentive and always precise, broke the silence with words full of love. "Imagine this, my love: a future where we fly together not only over distant beaches but over an entire lifetime full of adventures. Can you imagine it?"

"Yes, Elias. A future where we grow old together, but where we always find new ways to soar. Or new forms of adventure," replied Laila, with a smile that reflected the promise of her eternal love for him as she had proposed before God.

The gentle descent marked the end of their flight, but the experience would never end because it would forever be engraved in their hearts. Landing with their feet in the sand, they looked at each other. It was as if, immediately, the fact of having shared this adventure together, of having touched the sky, of accompanying each other at the top, in the eternal, made the connection between them grow a few inches deeper than it already was.

Feeling this way, they both understood the importance of "sharing." Of having goals, challenges, adventures, experiences, journeys, joys, and sorrows in common. Because it would be these things they could call "theirs" and that did not belong to singularity, that would make their love grow and strengthen.

"Thank you for giving me this dream, Elias," whispered Laila, embracing him with gratitude.

"There is nothing I wouldn't do for you, my love. And this is just the beginning of our adventures together," declared Elias, sealing his words with a tender kiss. The beach, witness to their flight, knew how to remain silent, but it would never forget that it was present when this young couple learned an important lesson and that their love continued to soar, like a paraglider taking flight with the infinite sky as its goal.

After landing and allowing the emotions to settle in their bodies and return to their places of origin, the spouses sat together on the sand. Both allowed themselves the small luxury of feeling the sun's warmth gradually accelerating with each passing minute.

They were grateful to feel the warmth on their faces, stripping away the cold that had accumulated in their noses.

"Can you imagine if we could live like this our whole lives?" asked Laila, intertwining her fingers with Elias's.

"I would love to. I would love to travel the world with you and then return home, wherever it may be located."

"One in Saltillo, another in Raouche, and we will always have Dubai. My parents' house in Dubai," Laila said, bursting into laughter as she tried to conceal it by covering her mouth with her hand.

"Very funny!"

"No, but I'm serious. I imagine having a house in the mountains, away from the hustle and bustle of big cities. If it's not too much to ask, I want the little house to have a sea view. I want to go to sleep and have the only sound be the whisper of the waves telling secrets to the cliffs before turning into sea foam," she replied, with a sparkle of anticipation and longing in her eyes.

"And our children running around on the beach, growing up with messy hair full of salt. Building sandcastles and flying kites when there are windy afternoons. Can you imagine it?" Elias suggested, with a radiant smile that almost didn't fit on his face.

"Yes. Of course, I can imagine it. In fact, I can see it as if I were watching a movie. I've even imagined much further."

"Oh really?" Elias asked with a hint of curiosity in his voice.

"Of course! I've even seen the movie of our grandchildren, about a dozen of them, sharing laughs and funny anecdotes with us in that little mountain house, which we'll fill with furniture, photographs, laughter, and memories," she added, embracing Elias tenderly, making sure there was no one on the beach who could look at them.

After a few magical days in Jounieh, the newlywed couple embarked on a long flight to Mexico. The plane, with their new home as the final destination, soared through the skies. For him, it was the long-awaited return home; for her, it was a completely new and exciting adventure.

As they flew above the clouds, Elias took Laila's hand and drew her closer to him to whisper a secret in her ear:

"Do you realize how far we've come? From that day we met, to now, flying together on the same plane and to the same place in the world. That world that now seems quite tiny from the window," Elias commented.

"Yes, and I wouldn't change anything about this story. Every moment, every adventure has been like a perfect chapter of our love story," Laila replied, resting her head on Elias's shoulder.

The sun sat on the horizon as the plane descended toward Monterrey. A bunch of little lights announced their arrival. The city stretched out before them, welcoming and full of memories. The journey back marked the beginning of a new chapter, where the magic experienced in Joünié began to look more like the most beautiful scene of a dream. And so, with the sun bidding farewell in the west, the wheels of the plane abruptly touched the runway. With that thunderous but reassuring sound, Elias and Laila knew that a new stage of their lives had begun. A new path to discover awaited them, but both sensed that it would be a journey filled with love, shared dreams, and the promise of growing old together, always with the sky as a witness to their eternal romance.

Chapter Twelve

An Encounter in Time

"To define a place as magical,

you need at least two people sitting together."

Fabrizio Caramagna

Elias couldn't resist the excitement of surprising Laila once again. Barely landing in Monterrey, upon their return from a wonderful honeymoon trip, he invited her on a mysterious road trip. Intrigue shone in Laila's eyes as he drove his black truck along winding roads and through landscapes that seemed to transform with every curve.

After rolling for just over an hour and spending those minutes sharing laughter, listening to good music, and chatting like two accomplices, Elias slowed down the car in a place that left Laila speechless. Monterreal stretched out before them, a corner of Mexico dressed in white during the early days of December. Snow covered the ground and the mountains, creating a wondrous landscape that seemed to be taken from a fairy tale.

"Are we going much further?" she asked, perhaps eager to know what Elias's surprise was all about.

"Laila, look to your right!" said Elias, pointing with his hand.

"I can't believe it... It's snow!"

"Snow in Mexico!"

"It's incredible! I didn't know we could find such a magical place in Mexico. And with snow," said Laila as she rolled down the car window to stick out her hands and touch the snow that was just beginning to fall shyly. A few flakes melted on the palms of her warm hands. "Why didn't you tell me about this place?" she asked curiously.

Elias smiled knowingly. "I saved this secret for a special occasion. I wanted our first adventure together, after the honeymoon, to be unique, and for your first days in my country to be unforgettable. A little gift before returning to routine and starting our 'normal' life."

"'Normal' life? I don't think we can have a 'normal' life. We are too fun and unconventional for that.

The spouses, now enthusiastic about the adventure they could predict thanks to the landscape surrounding them, sang along to the song playing inside the car. One of the Goo Goo Dolls' long discography and then, of course, their classic "Iris." Ten minutes later, Elias shouted her name, so that she could hear him even though the chorus of one of the songs was playing at full volume.

"Laila, we're here!"

Laila, excited, looked around, unable to contain her amazement. The cold of winter in the Sierra de Arteaga did not diminish the warmth she felt in her heart. Then she saw a small cabin made entirely of wood and stone that was hidden among towering snow-capped pines.

Later that night, wrapped by the same heavy wool blanket, they sat in front of the cabin's fireplace. One of the caretakers of the house had lit the fire and prepared everything, so now they were invited by the crackling of the burning wood and the warmth of the scene. Elias took Laila's hands, warming them between his own. The couple embraced, appreciating the stars that dotted the darkening sky through the huge windows.

"Imagine this, Elias," Laila said, laughing. "Imagine that the zombie apocalypse takes us by surprise while we're here in Monterreal, between mountains of snow and we're only illuminated by the stars in the sky. Do you think we would survive?"

"Ah, it's time for science-fiction-Laila. I like it! Well, the first thing," he said, trying to speak without being interrupted by his own laughter. "The first thing would be to find coats so our brains don't freeze and we can stay warm."

"Obviously. We don't want frozen brains. That point is covered, but... what do we do with the zombies?"

"I think," Elias responded thoughtfully. "I think we could exterminate them using an extreme and ancient sport."

"Which one?"

"Snowball throwing." Both laughed out loud.

"I like the idea," she said. "But what would we do if they start to corner us?"

"That's where my secret skill would be very useful," Elias said confidently, as if trying to inject some seriousness into the conversation.

"What is that skill that I don't know about yet?" Laila asked curiously.

"Sleds... Sleds for escape and to slide to our freedom."

"I have to admit, Elias, you have a perfect plan on your hands," she said, following the seriousness that had suddenly taken over the conversation.

"In addition, we have this cabin which is like an anti-zombie bunker. A perfect refuge. Have you seen the pantry? We have enough hot chocolate to survive for months. Plus, I saw that the TV room is stocked with an arsenal of movies. We're not going to get bored."

"That's for sure. Your company, chocolate, and movies sound like a perfect plan. In fact, I wouldn't wait for the apocalypse to come to put it into action."

"I couldn't agree more," he told her.

"So, to sum up. Basically, our strategy is to bundle up, throw snowballs, escape on sleds, and take refuge with hot chocolate."

"Exactly that," Elias replied, smiling from ear to ear. As if he wanted the science fiction fantasy to come true so he could spend time with Laila. "Can you imagine anything more romantic than surviving a zombie apocalypse together?"

As they drifted off to sleep in the cozy cabin, Laila and Elias couldn't help but smile at the thought of their future adventures, both real and imagined.

"I don't know, but I think we've found the perfect combination: love, laughter, and sledding in a world full of zombies," Laila mused.

"I've always thought our love is so strong that even the zombies would surrender to us," Elias replied as he wrapped his arms around her.

"All jokes aside, the truth is that being with you, here, surrounded by miles and miles of snow... It feels like a dream," Laila murmured.

"Yes, my love, but it's our dream," Elias said softly, sealing the moment in their hearts.

Night enveloped Monterreal with its dark, starry cloak, and the wooden cabin became a cozy refuge from the vast winter landscape. Laila and Elias, after a day full of laughter and adventures on the road, found themselves inside, embraced by the warmth of the fireplace.

With a passionate gaze, Elias took Laila's hand and led her towards the soft glow of the fireplace. The warmth mingled with the coolness of the night that seeped in through one of the half-open windows.

"Have you noticed how beautiful the moon looks tonight?" Elias whispered.

"Yes, it's as if the stars are celebrating something special," Laila replied.

Elias gently pulled her towards him, enveloping her in a tender embrace. The spark between them was palpable, like the air charged before a storm.

"I can't help but think how lucky I am to have you by my side, Laila," he said.

"The luck is mine, Elias. There's no other place in the world I'd rather be," she said as she stroked the back of his head.

The cabin, illuminated only by the dancing fire and the stars peeping through the window, created a magical scene that was uniquely theirs. The crackling of the firewood provided the perfect soundtrack for their connection.

Unhurried, Elias brought his lips to Laila's, exploring their love in a long kiss. They lost themselves in a warm embrace, where words dissolved and only their shared whispers remained.

The fireplace, a silent witness to their love, casted dancing shadows in the room. The flickering light chased away the cold from outside.

Guided by the deep connection they shared, Elias led Laila to a cozy corner of the cabin, where a soft blanket awaited them. Wrapped in the warmth of the fireplace and surrounded by the delicate, pure white snow that had fallen upon the wooden house, they let the heaviness of their eyelids lead the way, and both submerged into a deep sleep. The dialogues of a romantic comedy played in the background. Fatigue had prevented them from watching the movie.

The days of snow and romance in that cozy cabin were now a memory. Laila and Elias had returned to Saltillo, ready to make it their home. The city welcomed Elias with open arms, ready to witness their new life together.

With suitcases brimming with unforgettable moments, the couple headed towards Elias's apartment. This would be their first home for the first few months together. The apartment, located in a quiet residential area, became the blank canvas where they would begin to paint the first strokes of the masterpiece of their love. Elias, with a bundle of keys in hand, a bundle of nerves in his stomach, and a smile full of excitement on his face, unveiled the secret of the space that would be their home.

The apartment had a cozy atmosphere, with furniture that helped tell Elias's story and his days of solitude. There were also many details reflecting his taste for elegant simplicity. Laila admired every corner, absorbing the essence of her husband's former home, which now also belonged to her. The walls painted in warm tones invited calmness, and the large horizontal windows allowed natural light to fill the space with warmth. "There's such beautiful light here, Elias," she said.

"Welcome to our sanctuary, my love. This will be where we build all our dreams together," Elias said, looking at her with eyes full of genuine affection.

Laila nodded with an excited smile. Together, they began to unpack, placing carefully selected memories on shelves and in special corners. Each object had its story, and the apartment turned into a collage of their love.

The first weeks in Saltillo were a mix of discoveries and adjustments. Elias took Laila to the city's most iconic places, showing her his favorite spots and sharing stories from his childhood. Together they explored charming squares, colorful streets, gatherings with friends and family, and Elias made sure to introduce his wife to each of the dishes that were also part of who he was.

The nights were magical in their new home. They cooked together, as they had imagined since the moment, they did it through video calls. In the small but complete kitchen, they set out to try new recipes that merged the flavors of their cultures, delighting in candlelit dinners. Their complicity grew with each shared experience, sealing their connection in the small daily routines and the most unexpected details.

Elias's work and Laila's adaptation to her new environment filled their days with activities, but they always managed to carve out moments for reconnection. Weekends turned into small getaways to the nearby mountains, where they explored trails and got lost in the serenity of nature. Elias kept his promise, and finally, Laila got to know El Chiflón.

Over time, the apartment transformed into a true home, where both were thriving. And so, amidst the everyday routine and the magic that only love can weave, Laila and Elias wrote their story on the pages of Saltillo, building a future full of promises, laughter, and the certainty that together, they could face any challenge life threw their way.

Winter faded, making way for the scorching northern Mexican summer. The sun, freed from any restraint, poured its light onto the streets of Saltillo, seemingly intent on melting them. It was July, and the high temperatures, particularly for Laila, contrasted sharply with the pleasant cold of December when she first arrived at her new home.

One sweltering summer afternoon, excitement and laughter filled the air as the newlyweds headed to the bustling fairgrounds. Elias watched his wife with a smile full of enthusiasm. He was eager to share the vibrant traditions of his homeland. The Saltillo fairs, famous for attracting visitors from all over Coahuila and Mexico, were a colorful window into the local culture.

Happiness engulfed Elias as he showed Laila who he was, the roots that had shaped him. The fairs, with their explosion of color, mechanical rides, vibrant music, and exquisite food, were a perfect example for Laila to absorb the essence of Mexico.

As they ventured into the streets of downtown, the sound of parade music filled the air. Familiar notes for Elias, but fresh and exciting for Laila, who had everything to discover about her great love's life. With each step, they got closer and closer to the floats, the dancers, and the bands.

The vibrant colors of the stalls and the flickering lights began to illuminate in preparation to shine once the sun set. Children's laughter and the tinkling of traditional music filled the streets, creating a festive atmosphere that enveloped the couple in a knot of infinite happiness.

"Well, Laila, let me officially introduce you to the Saltillo fair. It's like a dream come true," Elias said, his eyes shining with excitement.

Laila nodded, amazed by the energy and joy that filled the place. "It's incredible, Elias. I've never seen anything like it."

They walked hand in hand, exploring the different stalls offering local delights: from grilled meat tacos to multicolored cotton candy. They stopped in front of a stage where local musicians played lively melodies that invited them to dance. "We can't miss the dance, can we?" suggested Laila, looking at Elias with a playful smile.

Elias took her by the waist, gently spinning her to the rhythm of the music. Surrounded by people who shared the same joy, they danced as if no one was watching. As best she could, she followed his lead, and they both joked about the clumsiness of their moves.

Satisfied from the fair's sights and tastes, they decided to visit Elias's parents. "The in-laws' house" was a recurring place in her new routine. It was a haven of peace, familiarity, and warmth. She felt like it was a piece of her home within this new and distant country. His family was beginning to feel like her own, and having them close helped heal her occasionally yearning heart, which sometimes missed the days in Dubai.

The family home was imbued with the aroma of traditional Mexican cuisine. Elias's mother greeted them with warm hugs and a table full of delicacies. "Welcome home, children!" exclaimed the mother, embracing Laila as if she had known her forever. She felt like her own daughter and loved having female company around.

The evening passed with laughter, shared stories, and delicious dishes. Elias's parents looked at the couple tenderly, noticing the complicity and love shining in their eyes.

While enjoying the family's hospitality, Elias reflected on the fortune of having Laila by his side, exploring together the traditions that were part of his identity. He was content and happy knowing that now, the Saltillo fair had become another chapter in the book of their shared memories.

Suddenly, Elias felt his cell phone vibrating in his pants pocket. He remembered the days, which now felt distant, when this was a signal that triggered a series of mixed emotions in him. Of course, when the message was from his love on the other side of the world. Elias didn't know that this message would also stir a jumble of emotions, even though, obviously, it wasn't from Laila.

Hassan_

Hello Elias. Son, how are you?

Do you have some time for us to talk?

It's important, dear.

Elias replied affirmatively to his father-in-law's text. He knew it was eight in the morning for Hassan and he was starting his day, so he preferred to get up from the table for a moment and take the call. He was now completely intrigued by that message.

The evening with the in-laws came to an end, and Laila and Elias, after saying goodbye warmly and showing gratitude for the food, returned to their little corner of the world.

It may sound like complete madness, but when you meet someone, that person has lived many lives before the encounter. This is a phenomenon that happens to both parties involved. Just for a moment, which can be paradoxically as ephemeral as perpetual, two souls cross their lives, their paths, their destinies, and then continue their course. He without her, and she without him. But for that moment, marked in memory, in history, and in existence, both souls shared a whole life in just one moment.

The evening with the in-laws came to an end, and Laila and Elias, after bidding farewell warmly and expressing gratitude for the food, returned to their little corner of the world.

It seems like complete madness, but when you meet someone, that person has lived many lives before the encounter. This is a phenomenon that happens to both parties involved. Just for a moment, which can be paradoxically as ephemeral as perpetual, two souls cross paths, share their destinies, and then continue their journey. He without her, and she without him. But for that instant that remains marked in memory, in history, and in existence, both souls shared a whole life in just one moment.

In the quiet of the night, Laila and Elias embarked on a conversation that went beyond time and borders. Words flowed like the whisper of the wind through the leaves of an old tree.

"Have you ever stopped to think about the transience of encounters in this life?" she asked.

"It's curious, isn't it? On the vast canvas of existence, our lives are just brief brushstrokes that intersect in time," he said thoughtfully, his gaze distant.

"Sometimes I wonder what stories and secrets the people we meet carry with them. As if each life were a book and we only had the chance to read one chapter."

"I like that idea, Laila. An infinite library of lives, and we only explore a few pages together."

"Isn't it crazy to think that we are like shooting stars in the vastness of the universe? We shine brightly for a moment and then disappear, but our light leaves a mark. A trail."

"Yes, Laila, each encounter is like a fleeting constellation. Two souls cross paths, share a moment, and then continue their journey."

"Just for a moment, your path and mine crossed, like two comets brushing against each other in the immensity of the cosmos. And even though we follow different trajectories, we shared a whole life in that encounter," she said, moved.

"I love to think that, even as our lives go on, we will always carry a piece of each other in our being. Like a treasure hidden in the deepest corner of the heart."

"It's as if our souls meet in an eternal dance, even when the dance in this physical plane comes to an end."

"And so, each encounter becomes an ephemeral work of art, painted with the unique colors of two intertwined stories."

Silence took hold of Laila and Elias's apartment. Then his voice, a gravelly voice that broke the silence, spoke.

"Hey, I don't know if you noticed, but during dinner at my parents' house, I got up for a moment to take a phone call."

"Yeah, I noticed. Is everything okay?"

"Yes. Everything's perfect. But the one who called was your father."

"Dad? Is everything alright?"

"Yes, Laila. Hassan called to offer me a job. A very good one, in fact."

"So, is this good news?"

"Well, it depends on how you look at it. Your dad called me with a job proposal. There's a vacancy to be a professor at the Beirut Arab University."

"BAU? Beirut Arab University?"

"That's the one," replied Elias. "Which means we have to move. But it also means we can be closer to your grandparents, your family, and it also means it's a great job opportunity."

"Is the Beirut Arab University the same one where my father has been teaching architecture classes online?"

"That's right. That's why he recommended me for the position. But in my case, the classes have to be in person."

"And your parents, Elias? Are we leaving them?"

"We can always come to visit or send them tickets to visit us in Lebanon. I think my dad will love the idea that his only son can rekindle a family dream by returning to the land where we're from, where my grandparents once left in search of new and better opportunities."

"If it's something that represents a dream and an opportunity for you, I'll always be by your side to support you."

"Thank you, Laila. Your opinion and support mean the world to me. Whatever we decide, we have to hurry. We have to be in Beirut in August, to be ready and trained for the start of classes in September."

Chapter Thirteen

Farewell

"(…) And I too dream and behold,

I dream I am bound with chains,

And I dreamed that these present pains

Were fortunate ways of old.

What is life? a tale that is told;

What is life? a frenzy extreme,

A shadow of things that seem;

And the greatest good is but small,

That all life is a dream to all,

And that dreams themselves are a dream."

Life Is a Dream, Calderon de la Barca.

Laila and Elias decided to take a tour around the city to bid farewell to the places that marked their days in Mexico. Despite the short stay, it was, after all, the first place that welcomed them as newlyweds. Amidst laughter, conversations, songs, and memories, they reached a high point in the city, a viewpoint that offered a breathtaking sunset over Saltillo. From this vantage point, it seemed like the privileged view belonged to them alone. It was a parting gift from this valley that first saw Elias grow, and then witnessed the love between them blossom.

Parked at the highest point, Elias remembered that this was the place he had always imagined enjoying a sunset with Laila from the moment he met her. Just as Elias had once fantasized during a flight back home, they both sat on the truck's bumper. Her honey-colored eyes met his in a look of love. Together, they were immersed in the shared enjoyment of the pink and orange clouds that, with their celestial brushstroke, painted the Saltillo valley at sunset, creating a scene of fleeting beauty. In silence, they enjoyed the colorful spectacle painting the sky.

Laila sighed and leaned on Elias's shoulder. "It's amazing how time passes so quickly. It seems like just yesterday when we arrived in Saltillo and now, we're about to leave for Lebanon." Elias nodded as he wrapped his arm around her shoulders. "It's true. It's been intense months, full of learning and many new experiences for both of us. But I won't deny that, although I feel some sadness about leaving Saltillo, I'm excited for everything I know awaits us in Lebanon. The Beirut Arab University is going to give us incredible opportunities, my love."

Night fell, and they both got into the truck to head to another destination. Elias's friends had been planning a surprise farewell party for the couple for several days. Elias and Laila had been summoned at 8:00 p.m. for dinner at his parent's house, but the smell of grilled meat that embraced the air on that night revealed that there were other plans in that house than just a formal farewell dinner. Roberto, Elias's best friend and the first to know about his great love, outdid himself with a gathering of friends and family. Garden, barbecue, good stories, laughter, and the best company. These were the kind of plans that Elias adored and knew he would miss a lot.

The night breeze gently caressed the corners of the house as Laila and Elias shared laughter in the backyard. Suddenly, a distant murmur began to fill the air, a melody hinting at an untold story. It was a melodic and vibrant sound, laden with the cultural richness of a mariachi band.

First, the sharp wail of the violin rose in the atmosphere, like a passionate whisper inviting joy. Its notes seemed to dance in the air, intertwining with the soft percussion of the guitars, resonating with a contagious rhythm, like the heartbeat of the party. Then the deep resonance of the guitarrón joined the ensemble, marking an exciting counterpoint that vibrated in the chest. Each pluck of the strings created a solid foundation, the bedrock of the impending celebration.

The trumpets made their triumphant entrance, sliding into the symphony with their festive flourishes. Every brass note resonated with vibrant clarity, as if the soul of the mariachi band was expressing itself in all its splendor. They were like rays of sunshine illuminating the scene, injecting energy and vitality into the moment. As the sound drew closer, the mariachi band's ensemble created a captivating symphony that filled the backyard. Laila and Elias's laughter mingled with the music, creating a magical moment where time seemed to stand still. The surprise of the mariachis' arrival manifested in every vibration of their instruments, weaving an unforgettable memory in the hearts of the couple and those present.

The musicians adjusted their hats, tuned their instruments, and suddenly, the expectant silence was interrupted by the vigorous sound of the trumpets. They began to play the unmistakable chords of "Cielito Lindo," a traditional Mexican song full of joy and optimism.

As the song progressed, the energy in the backyard came to life. People began to applaud to accompany the rhythm of the music, and some couples dared to dance, moving to the beat of the cheerful melody. Laila and Elias, surrounded by their loved ones, looked at each other with a complicity full of emotion.

The aroma of grilled meat wafted in the air, mingling with the music and creating a festive and unforgettable atmosphere. The mariachis continued to perform other traditional songs, creating a special soundtrack for Laila and Elias's farewell.

Tears of emotion soon appeared. The choice of "Cielito Lindo" not only brought the joy of the melody but also a nostalgic touch that reminded everyone present of the importance of family ties and the beauty of shared memories. That music, vibrating in their chests, felt "so much theirs" and made them feel like they belonged to something greater than themselves. That night, Roberto and the other friends made a pledge: to visit them in Lebanon someday, promising to keep the friendship alive despite the distance.

Elias's parents, Maria and Guillermo, were present at the emotional farewell, sharing hugs and good wishes with everyone. Elias's mother, with tears in her eyes, gave Laila a tight hug, thanking her for being part of her son's life and promising that she would always be welcome in their home. "You are the daughter I never had and always wanted," she said to Laila with a trembling voice, and she couldn't help but feel a strong desire to hug her deeply and return some love through her words.

These few days they had left in Saltillo would be intertwined with the excitement and anticipation of change and new opportunities. However, melancholy, sadness, and the void left by the goodbyes would also be present.

That night, Laila confessed to Elias that she felt Mexico in a deep place in her heart. "Who would have imagined that this country, which I only knew from references of very dramatic soap operas that reached Lebanon, would end up having a privileged space within my chest? These months we have spent here have been wonderful and will be forever engraved in my memories. Thank you for this, Elias!"

The day of departure finally arrived. María and Guillermo spent that cold and dark morning picking up Elias and Laila from their apartment. They wanted to drive to Monterrey airport to spend as much time together as possible before saying goodbye.

Tight hugs, words of encouragement, and promises of future reunions filled the moment. Laila confessed to her mother-in-law, "Although our stay in Mexico was short, I will always carry you in my heart. These memories, these wonderful people, will always be part of who I am, wherever I am. We'll be." Elias's parents hugged the couple amidst tears. They knew that Elias and Laila were embarking on a long journey and that their tickets had no return date. They were proud of their children's achievements, their strong union, and the decisions they had made. Yet, the heart is selfish when it comes to love, and the physical distance soon to separate them felt heavy.

Elias and Laila got out of Guillermo and Maria's white car.

As the plane soared through the vast sky, Laila and Elias settled into their seats, enjoying the relative calm of the first connecting flight that would take them from Mexico to Dubai. The dim lights of the plane created an intimate atmosphere, and the excitement of arriving in Lebanon, the final destination of the trip, mingled with the blessing of that moment just for them. To be alone and talk. One of their favorite activities as a couple.

Elias gently took Laila's hand, intertwining their fingers as they looked out the window at the city lights fading into the distance. Laila sighed, and Elias asked her lovingly, "What are you thinking, my love?" Laila smiled and rested her head on Elias's shoulder. "I'm thinking about our future, about everything that is to come. Sometimes, it scares me a little, but I know that together we can face any challenge."

Elias gave her a loving look. "We're a team, Laila. Always will be. I'm excited for what awaits us in Lebanon, at the Beirut Arab University. But I'm also excited to think about our future together and everything we're about to experience."

Laila nodded, looking at Elias with a mix of affection and curiosity. "Are you referring to... our children?" Elias pondered for a moment before responding. "Yes, I imagine so. I imagine a family very much in our style. Created in an environment of much love. I want to be a good father, teach them about our roots, about the value of diversity, and the importance of following their dreams." Laila smiled, imagining the future Elias described. "I imagine it too, Elias. I imagine watching our children grow, teaching them to love and respect, and sharing with them the stories of our lives. I want them to know where we come from and always have the freedom to be who they are."

Elias hugged her tighter, as if he wanted to envelop her in their shared dreams. "I don't care what comes our way, because as long as I have you by my side, everything will be alright. In fact, I know that together we will build a home full of love and happiness. And we'll always, always support each other every step of the way." Their conversation continued, delving into the clouds, the deepest dreams, and shared aspirations. As the plane advanced into the dark night, Laila and Elias found in those words a deeper connection, cementing their commitment not only to each other but also to the beautiful future they were building together.

After a long flight, Laila and Elias had arrived at Dubai airport, to await for a new flight with the final destination being Lebanon. That August night, Elias's wristwatch announced that it was 7:08 PM. The hustle and bustle made the conversation between the cosmic lovers more challenging than usual. "Do you feel like having a coffee? I'll go get something to drink," said Laila affectionately and smiling, almost shouting so he could hear her.

Elias nodded eagerly; with the same expression a child makes when asked if they want a treat. Then he parted his lips to try to pronounce a few words and tell her exactly what he was craving. Laila delicately placed her finger on them, as if trying to contain the words with the gesture. The delight of being able to afford these acts of physical closeness was incomparable, especially after so much waiting.

Knowing him perfectly, she felt that those brief words would be unnecessary. "Why do you tell me? I already know you're going to order an iced espresso," she affirmed with a smile. He winked at her and felt complete knowing that his soulmate knew him like the back of her hand.

Laila smiled at Elias before slipping through the crowd towards the nearest café in that terminal. Just like that August two years ago, they were both in the exact place where their love was born. Same boarding gate, same waiting area, same leather seats. It felt like déjà vu. In a mysterious corner of memory, *déjà vu* (from the French "already seen") unfolds like a momentary butterfly fluttering between the folds of time. That strange familiarity that shakes the mind is the nostalgic melody that resonates in the heart when the present merges with the past, like a delicate echo of another life.

The shadows of familiarity intertwine with the brightness of the unknown, creating a fabric in which memories and promises are eternally intertwined. Each moment of *déjà vu* is a suspended fragment in the ether, a glimmer of *déjà-rêvé* that whispers in the soul, reminding us that reality is just a veil separating what was from what is yet to be.

In those fleeting flashes, we are time travelers, navigating the currents of memory, where each repetition is a beacon, guiding us to the understanding that the past and the present are accomplices in the eternal dance of existence.

The promise of an iced espresso gave Elias the pleasure of experiencing one of those tiny everyday joys, which are as necessary as they are enriching. Just like the sound of ocean waves, waking up to the birds' chirping, tasting home-cooked food after a long journey, a steaming cup of coffee when you open your eyes in the morning, the invisible embrace of your "home" welcoming you, comforting words, and hearing an old song suddenly on the radio.

Elias settled into the plush brown leather chair and pulled his phone from his pocket. He glanced at the screen, noting the time, and also noticed an important notification. The work email he had been waiting for sent those familiar icy pangs through his stomach, reminiscent of the ones he had just felt moments ago when he thought he would be late for his flight, attempting to navigate through the modern steel and glass dome that shelters passengers from all over the world.

Helping the intrusive thought pass by, he grabbed his cell phone and began to swiftly move his fingers across the screen. With the help of his thumb, he tapped to open the email. He quickly read through the lines, as if trying to find the keywords that would give him a general idea of the response he wanted. Bingo! He had found what he was looking for, and in doing so, the pangs subsided.

He relaxed his body and let the tension slowly release from his neck. He took a deep breath. Then his thumb returned to play with the screen of his cell phone. He found Spotify. Among the top options was a song he had recently heard and loved.

He tapped the white circle and the melody began to play in his wireless headphones. He glanced at the clock on the screen. It was 7:11 PM. The masterful beginning of "*Júrame*", performed by Luis Miguel for his album "*Romances*", briefly made him close his eyes to focus on the moment he was experiencing.

Júrame que, aunque pase mucho tiempo

(Swear to me that, even though a lot of time passes)

Nunca olvidaré el momento en que yo te conocí

(I will never forget the moment I met you)

Mírame, pues no hay nada más profundo

(Look at me, because there is nothing deeper)

Ni más grande en este mundo que el cariño que te di.

(Or greater in this world than the love I gave you.)

Her figure emerged from among the crowd. With her hijab gently waving, and her gaze luminous like a beacon that lights up the darkness, she sat beside him.

In the vast theater of dreams, where stars and hearts intertwine in a cosmic dance, their destinies rose like two forbidden constellations. Laila and Elias, lovers in time, defied the rules of the universe with their fiery passion. Now, in the final act of this divine tragedy, the curtain falls on their ephemeral and never-lived love, leaving an eternal echo of desires in the firmament and the promise of a meeting somewhere beyond time.

Laila, despite the kilometers traveled and the horizons we never shared, we will always have that starting point that continues to pulse in my memory: the Dubai airport.

She was like a shooting star, a fleeting gleam in the darkness of my night. Her brief presence left a feeling of longing for something that never happened. Even now, remembering her makes me reflect on the ephemeral nature of casual encounters and the great void in my heart that can only be filled by her.

There, beneath the incessant flutter of desires and airplanes, I forged an entire universe in my imagination with you; a life that never happened, but that, like a shooting star on a clear night, left its eternal residue in the skies of my soul.

You and I will always have Dubai.

Epilogue

The Threads of Love That Weave the Universe

"I was reading my destiny inside

your eyes without knowing it."

Franz Kafka

In the symphony of time, where each note unfolds a story, invisible threads connect hearts destined to find their echo in the universe. These are the threads of love, intertwining destinies in ways as mysterious as the constellations in the vastness of the sky.

The Red Thread Theory, a belief that weaves through cultures like a river of tradition, speaks of souls connected before birth. Like strands in a cosmic tapestry, these threads stretch across oceans, traverse continents, and defy the constraints of time and space.

On this celestial loom, stories of destined love are woven as unique patterns, each telling the epic of two souls finding each other at the perfect moment. Distance, cultural barriers, the trials of time - all these obstacles are merely links in the chain of events leading to the encounter of two hearts beating as one.

The red thread is more than an invisible connection; it is a promise, a symphony resonating in the hearts of those who believe in the magic of true connections. Through shared joys and overcome sorrows, this thread not only binds but also strengthens, transforming each challenge into an opportunity for growth and love.

And so, as the stars paint their constant dance in the firmament, the threads of love continue to weave their enchantment on the canvas of existence. It may manifest in the warm embrace of a friend, the connection between parents and children, or the merging of souls who choose to walk the path of life together.

In the intricate web of destiny, the threads of love transcend the realm of romance, extending in multiple directions like the branches of an ancient tree. These threads are not limited to the romantic bond between lovers; they are magical threads that intertwine in the most everyday moments, woven into the shared experiences that define the fullness of existence.

The thread of love is an unbreakable support between parents and children, a connection that goes beyond biology and delves into the ocean of understanding and acceptance. This thread is the force that maintains family ties, guiding them through ups and downs. It's the joy shared in small victories and sorrows overcome together.

It is also present in the love between friends. It is the friend who understands without words, who shares laughter and tears. Friends are those threads that intersect in time, creating intricate patterns of friendship that withstand storms and celebrate sunny days.

Interestingly, here in Mexico, the land of my birth and the cradle of my culture, there is a special word to describe friends. The word *"cuate"* is a colloquial expression used to refer to a close friend or companion. It is an affectionate term that denotes a relationship of friendship and camaraderie.

Even more fascinating, the word *"cuate"* has indigenous roots, specifically in Nahuatl, the language of the Aztecs. In Nahuatl, the word *"coatl"* means serpent. Within the Aztec language, *"cuate"* was used to refer to twins or siblings who are born together, sharing the same space, just like twin serpents. This concept of duality and closeness was transferred to Mexican Spanish, where *"cuate"* evolved to denote a close friend or a companion with whom one shares experiences and establishes a special connection. This word is not only an example of how relationships intertwine, but also of how Mexican identity embraces and celebrates its indigenous roots in the very fabric of its everyday language.

Between parents and children, the bond transcends the barriers we know. It is the love that begins even before birth, a deep commitment that manifests itself in care, guidance, and support. Through challenges and triumphs, this thread is a constant reminder that no matter how far individual paths may lead, there is always a fabric that unites two or more people and connects them heart to heart.

In the merging of souls who choose to walk the path of life together, the thread of love becomes the fabric of the relationship. It can be the life partner who shares dreams and aspirations, or the mentor who guides on the journey of self-discovery. These threads are the alliances that illuminate the path, making the journey more meaningful when shared with those who share a similar vision.

Woven into the very fabric of the cosmos, these threads of love unfurl, forming a web that connects hearts in a cosmic dance. In each meaningful connection, whether between lovers, friends, parents and children, or souls who choose to share their paths, the red thread is a reminder that the magic of love is universal and manifests itself in infinite ways.

Destined love is the melody that plays on the heartstrings, reminding us that in the vastness of the cosmos, each of us is connected in some way. Though our individual stories vary in detail, they all share the common thread of the search for love, a bond that transcends the barriers of time and space.

May these threads of love find their purpose in the fabric of our lives, guiding us towards connections that enrich the soul and ignite the light in the darkest places. For, in the end, the red thread of destiny is more than a belief; it is the eternal poetry of love that unites us all in the perpetual dance of the universe.

وأتركك في رعاية الله

About The Author

Farid Mery Rojas

Farid Mery Rojas, born on December 11, 1987, in Saltillo, Mexico, is an author whose identity is woven between Mexican roots and the Lebanese cultural influences inherited from his father. This unique fusion has permeated his life and work with unparalleled richness, shaping his culture, his palate, and expanding his insatiable curiosity.

Since his childhood, Farid has been a tireless explorer, attributing his best quality to his curiosity. This quality has driven him to seek answers, to travel, and to discover the world around him. In his own words, he describes himself as "a 35-year-old, very curious child." Although initially inclined towards international trade, pursuing a Bachelor's degree in the field, the influence of his father and his desire to follow in his footsteps as a skilled merchant were evident. Perhaps influenced by the Arab cultural reputation in the business realm, Farid found his way to a Master's in Business Administration, thus solidifying his business acumen.

Contrary to the monotonous office life, Farid prefers to immerse himself in the outside world, establishing connections with people from diverse cultures. His network of contacts, acquaintances, and friends reflects his desire to be in constant contact with the diversity of colors, flavors, and scents that the world has to offer. This appreciation for cultural variety translates into his passionate love for traveling, a practice that fuels his creativity and enriches his works. With his pen, this author shares stories that reflect not only his cultural heritage but also his fascination with the interconnection between people and the experiences that arise from diversity.

His unique literary approach and dedication to exploring the nuances of life make him an author whose work transcends borders and resonates in the hearts of those who seek beauty in the complexity of the world around us.